Scary In Love

Holly June Smith

The characters and events portrayed in this book are fictitious. Any similarity to real persons, living or dead, is coincidental and not intended by the author.

Cover design by Aida Linnea @algart_

Sticker graphics by Meg Jones @megdesignedthis

Contents

A Note From Holly

Thank you for picking up Scary In Love. I hope you enjoy reading this spooky, spicy Halloween rom-com as much as I enjoyed writing it.

This book is a love letter to some of my favourite things: spooky season, old English country houses, women who feel like they don't fit in, and men who always make sure their partner comes first.

It is set in a fictional town in England, so unfortunately we cannot visit, and written in British English.

Scary In Love is NOT a dark romance, but if you would like Content Warnings for this book, you can find a list at the back.

If you prefer to skip them, you can jump straight into the queue for The Miller Mansion.

If you dare...

For Ellie and Emily

"All weird little creeps are welcome here."

– Mason Miller

1

Jenna

The Miller mansion sits far back behind imposing gates, high on a hill on the edge of our boring little town. It's run-down and creepy, and I fucking love it.

In a place like Crowmorne, where nothing ever really happens, everyone has a story about Old Man Miller. And since I've lived here my whole life, I've heard them all.

Some people say he was a wizard. Or a hermit. Or a criminal hiding out, keeping close guard of the millions he'd stolen in a bank heist that left him a wanted man. Some people say he had half a face, or eleven fingers. Some people think he was running a meth lab and a drug empire behind closed doors, and I think *some people* have seen too many movies.

Truth is, nobody really knows a thing.

When we were kids, my brother, Marcus, and I would hold our breath when we drove past the house, a superstition passed down by our parents. When we got older and bolder, we'd lurk by the gates with binoculars, hoping to catch a glimpse of a figure in one of the many, many windows. We never did, and to this day, we're still not sure what he looked like.

Nobody knows exactly when or how Old Man Miller died, either. Only that one day a private ambulance was spotted leaving, the gates were chained shut, and they stayed that way for years.

Until this past January, when the locked chains disappeared. A white transit van was seen coming and going at all hours, and gossip was rife.

"A famous director bought it, and they're shooting a film up there," Mum said. She knows everybody's business, so this was the most sensible theory by quite some stretch.

"It's a footballer and his supermodel wife," said Dad.

"It's neither," Marcus chimed in, nose buried in his cryptocurrency app. "An illegitimate son inherited the house and all the land that comes with it. Lucky fucker. Must be worth a fortune."

Over the summer, an advert in the newspaper invited locals and students at the nearby drama school to audition for a *'unique project'*. Mum doubled down on her film director story, but nobody, myself included, saw the place being turned into a tourist attraction.

A month ago, a banner appeared out front, and all became clear.

"Will You Survive The Miller Mansion?"

A link took me to a website promising a night of unprecedented access to one of the scariest houses in Britain. I bought tickets on the spot, and finally the night is here.

The enormous iron gates have been opened to the public after years of intrigue, and with spotlights illuminating the house from below, it looks creepier than ever.

The group of guys ahead of us in the queue squeal, and shriek, and whip each other into a frenzy. I'm just thrilled to be here.

Unfortunately, my date has yet to stir the same reaction.

Peter is a thirty-two-year-old tax advisor from nearby Bramwell. We met on a dating app a week ago, after I got bored and reactivated my account for the umpteenth time. His profile was all beige-flags; works from home, loves dogs, looking for someone to enjoy long walks in nature and pub lunches with. Average stuff, but it's a sad state of affairs out there and the dating pool is small. At this point in my life, if there are no red-flags, and I don't scare them off, I'll give them half a chance.

We had a drink in the *Sun and Stars* pub and the obligatory 'getting to know you more' chat before making our way up the road out of town. Apparently, he studied medicine at university before something *'utterly revolting'* made him pass out, then drop out. He's been in finance ever since.

This juicy tidbit was the first interesting thing he'd said, but no amount of needling would make him reveal what it was. Which is a real shame, because *'utterly revolting'* is kind of my whole vibe.

Ever since I was a little girl, I've been drawn to the creepy and weird. The spooky and unsettling. The deplorable and taboo.

My parents used to find me sneakily borrowing library books about ghost sightings and true crime on my Mum's adult-lending card. Or in the woods behind our house, rooting around in the dirt, lifting rotting logs, and hunting for bugs. Or digging up my pet rabbit to study the various stages of decomposition.

Okay fine, I will accept that one is quite weird.

As a teen, I was interested in death and anatomy, the history of the occult, voodoo, and ritual ceremonies.

'Why can't you be normal?' Mum used to despair, but this *was* normal to me.

The fox's head was the final straw. I was keeping it in a bucket of water in the back garden, waiting for Mother Nature to do her thing and leave me with a beautiful clean skull to add to the collection on display in my room. I already had a few birds, and a rat, but I wanted that fox so badly. Dad puked in Mum's dahlias, and she hit the roof and sent me to a therapist.

After three months of sessions, she concluded there was nothing wrong with me. I was simply a curious child who should perhaps consider a future career in taxidermy or forensics.

Thanks, Hilary. You're a real one.

Despite those words of encouragement, I still strongly prefer the company of the living. After school, the obvious choice was to work at Crowmorne Heights, the retirement home my parents run. Twelve years later, I've worked my way up to Senior Care Manager, my relationship with them is much stronger, and I can't imagine doing anything else.

The residents I work with are a fucking riot, some of the most brilliant, funniest people I've ever met, once you give them time to warm up to you. And while they're still with us, of course.

When you see these things as often as I do, you stop being afraid of death or dying. I'm far more terrified of things in the real world, like the persistent dismantling of basic human rights by those in power, urinary tract infections, and falling in love.

I wonder what Peter would have to say about that last one, but he hasn't actually asked me a single question about myself tonight. Now I'm playing a game where I wait and see how long it takes for him to turn the conversation in my direction.

It was my idea to visit the Miller house for our first date. Figured I'd throw him in at the deep end, and see if he's worthy of my time. He seemed open to it, but judging by the blank look on his pasty face, he's not gonna be the man to match my freak.

2

Mason

This is really happening. Opening night of The Miller Mansion, the sleepy town of Crowmorne's first Halloween haunt.

In the backstage break room, the forty-strong cast and crew I've assembled and trained over the last few months are in high spirits.

Some are locals, some are London friends I know from acting circles, but all have two things in common. One, they *love* Halloween. And two, the future of this house depends on them.

They all know the backstory. I've stayed upbeat, haven't wanted to put pressure on them, but the worries I've been burying for months are creeping back in.

I've worked a lot of haunts, but this is my first time running one, and I'm functioning on caffeine and adrenaline at this point. It's occupied every waking thought, and plenty of sleeping ones, since I had this ridiculous idea six months ago.

Now it's time to find out if it's all been worth it.

"Okay, team, I need all eyes on me and just a minute of your time." They huddle closer and their chatter dies off. "Hey, Nicky, over here."

"I'm looking at you, boss. My custom contacts point in different directions."

I snap my fingers and point at one, then the other. "Right! I keep forgetting. Those are outstanding, by the way."

Nicky is one of several actors who play the staff of the Miller house. Their job is to roam the hallways, gently spooking but mostly guiding customers from one space to the next. Our scare teams will run each room, and they're responsible for giving guests the fright of their lives, but Nicky and the hands-off crew are the backbone of making an experience like this a success.

We don't want guests going rogue or wandering off into spaces out of sequence. Every haunt operator has stories about customers who are determined to go off-script, desperate to peel back the curtains, literally in some cases. Some people try to scare us before we can scare them, but I'm confident this lot will be the only ones scaring.

"We open in ten minutes. Your costumes look amazing, your make-up is incredible and terrifying. You've trained hard for this, and I know you are all gonna kill it tonight. Metaphorically speaking. We're here to have fun, but we also have an important job to do. So what's our motto?"

"Scaring is caring!" the team shouts in unison.

Everyone is buzzing for opening night, but it's a little weak for my liking.

"I know it seems corny, but I'm gonna make you do this briefing every single night, so we never forget it. People come here for a very specific experience, and we're all here to make sure they get it, so let me hear it louder, in character."

I cup my hand to my ear, and they yell, shriek, roar, and howl back at me.

"Scaring is caring!"

"That's right. We scare the first person through that door just as hard as the last. I'll be based in the Tavern supporting the bar crew all night, but I have my earpiece in if you need anything. Have a great time, and I'll see you all back here after closing for pizza and beers."

They file out, heading off to the different parts of the house we've worked so hard to set up for tonight, but I head in the opposite direction.

I want to lurk at the top of the grand staircase and watch the first groups of guests arrive. I need to see the anticipation on their faces, need to know this was the right call.

If tonight, and the next twenty, go well, then this crazy plan might just work.

3

Jenna

At the front gates, a young woman in a huge black parka scans our tickets and fastens neon passes around our wrists.

"You're all set," she says enthusiastically. "Please note photography and filming are not permitted inside the house. Please stick to the designated route, and in the event of a fire alarm, all lights will come up and our staff will lead you to the nearest exit. Make your way up to the main doors and get ready for the fright of your life."

A looming figure in a floor-length hooded cloak stands nearby, their outstretched arm holding a lantern to guide our way. Their face is hidden by a shiny silver mask and I find the whole thing pretty hot. The mask kink girlies are getting fed right away, it seems.

Advertising for this event has been minimal, so I'm really not sure what to expect when we get up there in terms of a haunt concept. What exactly are we trying to survive behind these walls?

"Isn't this exciting?" I say to Peter, who's grown terribly quiet by my side.

He shoves his hands deep in his coat pockets. "You really like all this haunted house stuff?"

Er, yes. If you paid an ounce of attention to me, you'd notice.

I keep that thought to myself. Can't expect a man to do something as groundbreaking as observe my body language on the first date. How silly of me.

Haunted houses and scare mazes started popping up all over the country about ten years ago. These seasonal events are big business, designed to lure in freaks like me during those quiet months before family-friendly Christmas markets and Santa's grottos take their place.

They're often set up on big farms, or industrial warehouses, blank spaces that are tailored to the design of each experience. Asylums full of zombies who've escaped quarantine, farms where scarecrows come to life and chase you across pumpkin patches, Blair Witch-esque forests, and good old-fashioned ghost houses. I've done them all.

The best haunts are the ones where the actors are big and intimidating and get right up in your face. So yes, I guess I really do like all this haunted house stuff. Having one open in our town, in such a unique and mysterious setting, is even more exciting.

"I love them," I tell him.

"Why?"

Wow, a question at last! Be normal. Don't spook the man before you've even made it inside.

"I like the fear, the panic, the jump scares. That moment when you think you're about to die, but you're actually fine. All that adrenaline is such a rush, don't you think?"

Peter screws up his face, and we continue walking.

Good job, Jenna. Not.

A lot of these places go to great lengths to decorate the approach to the main event and build anticipation. I've seen fake bodies hanging from trees, battered signs warning us to *'keep out'*, trails of fake blood on the ground as if someone has recently been dragged away.

Here, they've kept things simple. Fog machines and orange lighting make the house look even spookier than usual. From hidden speakers, music drones with the sounds of howling wind and birds cawing. In the trees that line either side of the driveway, fake crows stare down at us, their eyes glowing red.

I watch carefully as the group before us heads inside, screaming at whatever awaits them behind the heavy wooden door. It slams closed behind them, and Peter flinches.

"Are you ready?" I ask, holding my palm out for him to take.

I'm curious whether he's the type of man who sees himself as a protector, or if he'll be vulnerable enough to allow me to protect him.

"No," he says, keeping his hands in his pockets. "You knock."

It's official. Peter is a wet blanket.

He cowers behind me while I raise my hand to press the old bell, and when the door slowly creaks open, the sound effects are all real.

From the shadows inside, a small man appears before us. Like all these events, I'm instantly looking for signs of makeup and costume, the things that make or break these experiences. A bad costume will have me snapping out of the fantasy real fast.

He clears his throat as if it's full of dust. Short and scrawny, with long, white, stringy hair, he has a pallid complexion that makes him difficult to age.

"Come on in then," he grunts. "If ya dare."

"I don't dare," Peter whispers behind me. I grab his arm and drag him over the threshold.

"Come on, it'll be fun."

Just as I'd seen with the previous group, the door slams shut, and from somewhere a speaker plays the obligatory haunted house music. So far, so obvious.

There's a ghostly noise behind us, and Peter leaps about three feet into the air. "Oh my God, what the fuck?"

"Feeling brave, are we?" our host cackles. "Think you'll be the special little snowflakes who'll survive the Miller Mansion?"

He grunts again and shuffles closer, sniffing at the air between us. Peter hides behind me.

"No," he says. "We're nobody special."

Er, speak for yourself, mate. I'm a bloody delight.

"They should have left this place locked, you know? All you disgusting people, desperate to stick your noses in where they're not wanted. None of your stinkin' business what goes on here. You're the real ghouls."

The man lifts his lamp, casting a glow across the floor as he heads deeper into the grand entrance hall. I look up and take in our surroundings.

All my life I've wondered what lies beyond those gates, and I can't believe I'm actually inside the Miller house. This space is dark and dusty, with high ceilings and a huge chandelier covered in cobwebs. Those are definitely real.

This is my dream home aesthetic. I could quite happily spend my days flouncing around a place like this with only ghosts and spiders for company.

A carpeted staircase winds around one wall to the upper levels, and I crane my neck to see where it leads. At the top, a man in a shirt and waistcoat paces back and forth, whistling to himself as he swings an axe up onto his shoulder.

When our gazes snag, he does a double-take, and his axe falls to his side. I smile up at him, unsure if he's a background actor or someone we're supposed to acknowledge.

He leans against the balustrade and smiles back, full of cocky bravado I'm not normally into. Yet, when he tilts his head and casts his eyes down my body, I feel like I'm blushing all over.

His *Peaky Blinders*-style costume is hot, and so is his face. Definitely not from around here. On closer inspection, his hair is a mess, there's a bloody gash on his cheek, and he's still staring.

I give him a demure little wave, and he laughs to himself, pressing his tongue into the side of his cheek. Then he lifts one hand, points straight down at me, and draws slow circles with his finger.

Interacting with scare actors is the best thing about these haunts, and I love being told what to do, but this one feels different. Still, I follow his orders and twirl for him, blushing harder knowing he's studying me from all angles.

At the end of my rotation, I make eye contact and curtsey. When he sweeps his hand down his face, I lose all interest in the house. The only thing I want to know about is this guy.

4

JENNA

MY FEET HIT THE first step without thinking, but someone grabs my arm and pulls me back.

"What are you doing?"

"Huh?"

Oh. Peter.

The man I'm on a date with. Oops.

I drag my eyes away, and give Peter's hand the same reassuring pat I give my residents when they're frustrated their favourite TV show has finished.

When I look back, the man with the axe is still staring, but I lose sight of him when our guide leads us into a dark corridor.

"Don't follow him," Peter hisses.

"Peter, this is it. It's started. We're supposed to follow him."

"Hurry up," the guide barks at us.

We scurry along and try to stay close, but he stops short, snarling over his shoulder when we crash into the back of him.

"I suppose you'll want to know who I am then?" he huffs, then imitates a hacking cough right over Peter's shoes. At least, I think it's fake.

"Yes, please," I nod eagerly.

"I'm not him, if that's what you're thinking. Jessop's the name. Been working for the Miller family for as long as I can remember, you know? Seen it all. Heard it all, too." He leans in close. "Every wicked word. Even when they think I'm not listening, I am."

He taps the side of his nose and gives me a conspiratorial wink.

"And trust me, we know all about your gossiping and yammering about *'Old Man Miller'* all over town, but none of you really knew, did ya?"

Weaving the fictional experience with the very real and mysterious lore is a smart move. I still have no idea what's about to happen.

"All these years you thought there was just one man living here, but there was a whole family for a time, and they're just waiting to meet ya. Look."

He beckons us into a dim hallway, lifting his lantern to illuminate a gallery wall of family portraits. Men, women, children. The attention to detail is incredible.

"Lady Miller was beautiful, wasn't she?" he says, hovering over a wedding day portrait. "Was the best wedding we'd ever seen round these parts. Everyone agreed. Picture in the paper and all."

I follow him, studying the portraits closely, captivated by his storytelling. I swear one painting blinks, and I hold my breath to see if it does it again.

"The good Lady had a sister move in with her, the husband too, and there were children. Oh, so many children. Should have been a blessing, but Miller, well, he was never much of a people person. And he just loved 'em so much he wanted to keep 'em all for himself. Tucked away and out of reach of the evils of this world. Closed the curtains. Locked the doors. The boy—"

"What boy?" I ask, and he whips his head round.

"Oh, wait until you meet the boy," he cackles. "Never seen the light of day. So pale you'd think you'd seen a ghost. Floats around this place, all quiet like. But his thoughts? They're dark as pitch, and if he catches you..."

Peter makes a mewling sound. "I don't want to be caught by the boy."

"You'll never hear him coming," Jessop tells us, his voice turning sinister as he waggles one haggard, bony finger in our faces. "But he's not the only one you want to watch out for. You see, terrible things happen to people when they're hidden away their whole lives. Their bodies may be long gone, but their poor, poor souls... They'll be stuck here forever."

"Jesus Christ," Peter mutters.

"Jesus won't help you here," Jessop snaps. "This could have been a house full of love and happiness and laughter, but old Miller messed with their heads. Turned 'em cruel and wicked. Spiteful and mean. Tricksters, the lot of 'em. And they love to play games, so tread carefully."

He takes a step towards us. Peter takes two back, but I refuse to move, even though my adrenaline is thumping. I love this.

"Best keep your wits about you, and a word of warning that you didn't hear from me. Whatever they offer you, say no. These are people who'll be kind to your face while spittin' in your tea. Oh, they'll take offence, no doubt, but they've no respect for themselves, or each other. And definitely not for the likes of you, Miss."

He leans in close and sniffs my neck. My pulse sings. I'm not turned on by this guy, but I'm definitely stimulated in other ways.

It's not that it's sexy, but it is intimidating, and like I said, I'm a revolting creep. The line between fearing getting hurt and being excited by the loss of control isn't so much a line, but a big grey expanse for me. I hold my head high, defiant, and a small smirk appears on his face.

"Oh yes, the eldest son will love you."

He does the same to Peter, and for the briefest second, I think he's about to lick his cheek. Haunt actors are strictly hands off, but good ones will make you forget that and play on your fears.

"And you," he sneers. "You keep your filthy hands to yourself or you'll never see the sky again."

"I want to go home," Peter says.

"You are home," Jessop drawls, moving behind us and hustling us along to the end of the corridor. "Go on then. You mustn't keep the lady of the house waiting."

Peter refuses to budge, so I shove him ahead of me.

"I don't want to go in there," he whimpers, and I roll my eyes.

Yep, I'm definitely the protector here.

"Peter, it's fine. Nothing bad will happen to us. It's all acting, remember? Just stay close behind me."

"Hold my hand," he says, grabbing mine.

This would be cute if he didn't look like he was on the verge of tears. And if his palm wasn't drenching mine in his cold, clammy sweat.

5

Jenna

Peter squeezes hard as the door creaks open and we step into a musty, old drawing room.

Houses of this age are so big, most rooms have several doors through which to enter and leave. It makes them perfect for haunts because visitors can follow a loop through the property without ever seeing any other guests. Though that doesn't mean you won't hear their screams.

I've been to enough of these houses to know the scare actors always come from behind you, usually while you're distracted by something, or *someone*. As soon as the door closes, I'm glancing at the shadowy spaces for hidden figures, or curtains that drape so low they could definitely conceal a figure or two.

Some houses build fake walls with hidden doors for actors to hide behind, poised and waiting to strike. There are plenty of spots in this room, and I have to find a balance between anticipating the scares and relaxing enough to let it unfold around me. It's not as much fun when you've predicted everything that will happen.

This room is enormous, and I feel like I've stepped back in time. Maroon walls and ceilings, with gilded cornices I'm sure once gleamed in the sunlight. Brass wall sconces cast soft light down the walls, but the rest of the room is in darkness, save for the blazing fire.

Two sofas face each other, with a low table between them. We appear to have walked in on afternoon tea, but Peter and I are completely alone, which means someone will leap out on us at any second.

"What do we do now?" he asks.

A record crackles from an old gramophone in the corner.

"Now, we wait. Are you okay? Are you enjoying—"

A door at the opposite end of the room opens, and a woman with elegantly coiffed hair and a corseted dress interrupts us. Her face is powdery white, cheeks heavily rouged. She appears to float in with a tight smile on her face.

Peter shifts behind me. It was a stupid question. He's obviously not enjoying himself, but I am.

"Guests!" the woman cheers, clapping once and clasping her hands at her chest. "Oh, beloved guests. Welcome, please do come closer. Won't you join me for tea by the fire?"

"Nope," Peter says, popping the P.

Palming the small of his back, I guide him over to where the lady awaits, her smile just a smidge too wide. I take a seat on the sofa, tugging on his sleeve until he does the same.

Another man might shuffle closer because he can't bear to be even three inches away from me, but Peter scoots right up close because he's a wimp.

His thigh presses against mine, and the hairs on the back of my neck stand on end, but not because of him. Every nerve in my body knows that sitting on a sofa in the middle of the room means someone is going to approach us from behind.

They might barge in screaming, or sneak up in silence, but either way, I'm ready. I fold my hands in my lap and settle into the scene.

"Goodness, it's been so long since we've had visitors," she says, her posh British accent hitting all the right notes. "I had a strange feeling this morning that we'd be receiving visitors. I couldn't tell if it was a dream or a premonition. I said as much to my husband, the good Mr. Miller, upon waking."

With a soft hum, her excitement wanes, shoulders sagging as the flames draw her attention. She is silent for a long moment, her breath hitching before she speaks again.

"He scolded me for indulging in such fantasies, of course, and I paid the price. But afterwards, I had Sally prepare a few treats for us to enjoy, just in case. It really has been far too long."

So Mr Miller is a villain in all of this. I make a mental note to give him my best death stare when we meet him.

Lady Miller hums softly, leaning forward to lock eyes with mine. "How have you been, my dear?"

"I have been well," I tell her, playing along.

"Your new companion is most handsome." Her nose wrinkles, and she taps her fingertips together excitedly.

"Me?" Peter croaks.

"Oh yes. Jenna's previous acquaintances have left rather a sour taste." My back stiffens. "It is Jenna, isn't it? My memory isn't what it once was."

I nod politely, wondering how on earth they've managed to keep track of our names, and Peter's head snaps towards me.

"Do you know this woman?"

"No, I've never been here before."

"Nonsense!" Lady Miller snaps, her booming voice sucking all the air out of the room. "Why would you tell such filthy lies, girl?"

"I'm... sorry?"

I'm not sorry. I'm fucking delighted at being told off. Her tone sends a humiliating thrill up my spine.

"You will be," she mutters, her top lip curling in disgust before she fixes her smile back in place. "Tea?"

Peter and I speak at the same time.

"Yes, please."

"No, thank you."

At least he's remembered his manners.

"You'll drink my tea," she says, her voice so stern it makes me pinch my lips closed.

Thin brown water pours from the teapot. I watch for steam, a sign that it's authentic and hot, but I imagine from a health and safety perspective that's not possible.

"Milk."

It's not a question. She raises the jug, tilting it just so. Thick, creamy clumps of rancid slop land in the cup, splashing tea over the side.

My throat closes up, and beside me, Peter almost loses the contents of his stomach, retching over the side of the sofa.

I stifle a laugh and catch Lady Miller's eye. To her credit, she remains in character, frowning in disgust. She sets the teacups and saucers down, and lifts a three-tier cake stand from beneath the table, setting it in front of us.

Beyond the fact that the contents are inedible, there's a mutual understanding we won't actually interact with her props.

"Do help yourself. Everything was baked fresh this morning. Just for you."

Lady Miller's true title should be Queen of Bullshit. We lean in closer to see her *'fresh'* cakes are covered in green fluffy mold, I assume not real.

"Is something wrong?" Her smile is saccharine but deadly. "You wouldn't offend me by refusing my fine fare now, would you? Take a scone, dear."

I lift one to find it teeming with maggots. Peter gags into his hands and slumps against the back of the sofa.

The whole thing is perfect, and I've been so thoroughly absorbed in the scene, I don't notice a figure approaching behind us until he roars between our faces.

"The Lady said eat!" he roars.

It all happens so quickly. I drop the scone on the table, make my apologies and stand, ready to head for the next room. Peter leaps up, but the next thing I know he's on the floor, kicking and screaming like an upturned bug. If I didn't already have the ick, I definitely do now.

I look down to see an arm reaching out from underneath the sofa, shackling his ankle as he thrashes around. He's so loud I have to cover my ears, but when I stoop to help him up, his eyes shut so tightly he doesn't understand it's me.

"Leave me alone," he cries, his feet kicking out as he tries to escape the actor's firm hold. One connects with my knee, sending searing pain shooting through it.

"Motherfucker," I yell, hopping on the other leg before toppling backwards onto the sofa. Would be more apt if it were a Victorian fainting couch.

"Oh shit," Lady Miller says, dropping her accent as she rushes to my side. Peter scrambles towards the door we first came through.

"Get out of my way," I hear him yell, leaving me alone with three actors whose shocked expressions are definitely not part of the act.

6

Mason

The Tavern is the spot guests arrive in immediately after exiting the haunt. It's a place to decompress after the horrors of the main event, and I've pulled old furniture from all over the house to make sure they can relax and enjoy Halloween-themed drinks.

It's also where I'll spend most of the night, a base to make sure everything is going as planned. The cast and crew have rehearsed each scene often enough that I'm confident it will take guests one hour to make their way through all our rooms, but tonight I can't focus. I'm too busy watching the door, hoping the mystery beauty from the bottom of the stairs will walk through it soon.

It's still early.

She'll turn up eventually.

Staff in the Tavern wear 1920s outfits: tweed suits, club-collar shirts, and flat caps. With bloody faces and an assortment of weapons, we've obviously been brawling, though it's not clear if we're the victims or the instigators. Our well-rehearsed lines should keep guests guessing until the doors close at eleven sharp.

My weapon of choice is an axe with a long wooden handle, a dummy prop that makes a great addition to the bartending experience when I smack the butt down on the bar top, or serve carefully balanced shots off the flat side of the head.

Sammy has a pistol, Lulu has a blade hidden down the front of her corset, and she'll do a great bit, whipping it out when it's time for customers to pay up.

Given how much an alcohol license and security cost, I'm hoping we'll make plenty of extra cash through the bar, and we want people to stay as long as possible.

Everything is on schedule until my radio earpiece sparks with the one thing no haunt director ever wants to hear.

"Medical assistance required in the drawing room. Medical assistance required in the drawing room."

I push the button to talk and grab a first aid kit from underneath the bar. "On my way."

My pocket watch is an authentic part of my costume, which luckily still works. We've only been open for twenty minutes. How can we have a first-aid incident already? And in the drawing room, of all places? All guests have to do is walk in and sit down.

My brain whips through the details of the room. Two sofas, one table, no trip hazards, one—

Oh shit. The fireplace.

When I drew up our risk assessment, necessary for both a safe experience and insurance purposes, I knew the open fire would be deemed high risk. But I have safety protocols in place; a fireguard, extinguishers, and a room crew who know to keep guests away from open flames. That brought the risk down to medium, but if someone's been burned, I'll never forgive myself. It'll be the end of haunt season, and my time here too.

First-aid instances aren't unheard of in scare houses. Usually, it's a fainting guest, and we take them to a bright, modern room for a cup of tea and reassurance that it was all made up and everything will be absolutely fine.

If it's not a burn, and Clarissa's made someone faint in the very first room, then she deserves a bonus.

"Ron, hold the next group until I give you my word," I say through my earpiece.

"Copy that."

In his role as Jessop, the butler, it's Ron's job to greet our guests and help them enter the house on time. He sets the scene for the story, but he's also a master at making stuff up on the spot, and I'm sure he can entertain them for a few minutes.

It took a while to learn the layout of the house, but I know every inch now, even in the dark. I weave through the corridors that are closed off to the public and get there in under thirty seconds.

As per protocol, the team has turned the lights up, and stepped out of character to support our guest. Though in these costumes, you wouldn't know it.

Every room has a mix of interactive actors, the ones who tell their part of the Miller family story, and scare actors. Their role is fairly self-explanatory. One of those will be the room lead, and it's their responsibility to make sure everything runs smoothly. Through rehearsals, they form a tight-knit crew who will scare and reset, over and over again, every night for the three weeks we're open.

When I burst into the drawing room, I find Clarissa and Matteus, our Lady Miller and our scare actor, huddled around the sofa but no sign of Mikey.

They step aside to reveal the guest, reclining on our sofa, clutching her knee, chest heaving as she breathes deeply.

Her.

The woman at the bottom of the stairs.

The most beautiful woman I have ever seen.

It takes great effort to pull my eyes away, but I scan the room for signs of blood, or hazards that could injure someone else. She's clearly breathing, and nobody is on fire, thank fuck.

"It's her knee, boss," Matteus says, stepping aside to let me crouch in front of her. My hands reach into the kitbag for an instant icepack while I attempt to check her over.

It's a top-to-bottom process, starting with scanning for a head injury, but my thoughts get lost in the long dark waves spilling over her shoulders, and the bleached blonde streaks that frame her face.

Just like before, my instinct is to curl them around my fingers and pull her close, but I focus on squeezing the pack, shaking it to activate the cold while I keep going.

My gaze travels from her dark brown eyes to full, pouty lips, then down to where the buttons on her cardigan strain against her cleavage. It's cropped, revealing a band of bare skin above the pink skirt she's paired with black ankle boots, and those fishnet tights.

I'm fucked.

Fishnets are my weakness.

Not only do they look incredible stretched over her gorgeous thighs, but they're the super sexy kind with big, wide gaps. The perfect size for me to hook my fingers into and rip apart.

Always wanted to. Never had the chance.

The tights caught my eye when she first walked in. Instead of hiding her body, they beg me to look, and the rest of her is just as stunning. Motioning for her to spin around for me wasn't strictly part of my act. I did it without thinking and hadn't expected her to actually do it.

"You..." she whispers.

"Yeah. Me."

Women have been the last thing on my mind while I've been preparing for tonight, but this one has my full attention.

I can't look away, and she's looking back, her eyes bouncing around my face as she checks out my makeup. The bruised eye, busted nose, and bleeding cheek, all fake of course, but convincing enough thanks to lessons from the specialist make-up artist I hired to train the cast.

"Can I?" I ask, holding the icepack closer to her knee. She nods and pulls her hand away. Her skin looks red and tender.

I cup the back of her calf to hold her steady, and press it gently against her. She hisses at the contact, then throws her head back with a breathy moan that's probably pained but definitely sounds like pleasure.

Still on one knee, I watch as her lower lip disappears behind her teeth, and she moans again. I press harder. Goosebumps prickle up her thigh, and the tip of one of my fingers slips beneath a strand of her fishnets.

She squeezes her eyes shut. Her legs part ever so slightly. I stroke the soft skin at the back of her knee. She shudders, and time stands still, until Clarissa coughs behind me, snapping out of whatever the fuck I'm doing here.

"I'm so sorry," I tell our guest before reluctantly dragging my gaze away from her to talk to the crew. "What happened here?"

"It wasn't me."

A balaclava-clad face appears beside my thigh, and Mikey rolls himself out from underneath the sofa. It was his idea to use a car creeper, a board on wheels that helps him slide in and out, and it was a damn good one.

"Really, it wasn't their fault," she winces, her lips pinched together as she breathes through the pain. "Your cast are excellent. It was my date. He freaked out and kicked me."

I look around the room for the dickhead who did this to her.

"Then crawled out of here on his hands and knees looking like he was about to piss himself," Matteus says.

The woman laughs, a beautiful sound, then winces as she tries to sit upright.

"Well, in that case, job well done, team. I'll take it from here."

They hurry to reset the room, ready for the next group.

"I'd really love to check you out a bit more."

She smiles at the unintended innuendo, and my brain short-circuits for a second, picturing her lying back, skirt hiked up, with me on my knees for other reasons. I squeeze her calf one more time, reluctant to let go.

"Your knee, I mean. Check it out in our first aid room? It's not far. Do you think you can walk?"

"I can try," she says, taking hold of my arm and pushing up onto her feet.

7

Jenna

I COULD PROBABLY HOBBLE on my own, but it's much nicer to lean into this tall, handsome stranger who smells utterly divine.

His costume is smart navy trousers and a matching waistcoat, over a white shirt he's rolled up at the sleeves. On first impressions, he's dapper, but when you look closely, he's a little rough around the edges. His shirt is grubby and torn at the collar, and his face is a bloody mess, I assume from a scuffle.

Quite the mental image. Trust me to get horny thinking about two dudes fighting.

I grip his elbow, and he juggles carrying his kit bag and his axe in the other hand. I hadn't noticed he was still carrying it when he first appeared on the scene, and why would I? All I could focus on was the face of the man on his knees in front of me.

If I hadn't been in so much pain, I'd have hooked a leg over his shoulder and pulled him closer without thinking.

"What's the axe for?" I ask.

"Oh, you know. Breaking and entering, chopping my enemies into pieces, that sort of thing."

"Who are you supposed to be?"

"Oh, I'm sorry, I should have introduced myself. I'm Mason."

"Mason Miller." I try to remember his portrait from the family gallery, but I'm certain I'd remember this face. "Are you The Boy?"

"No," he laughs softly. "I'm Mason. Are you sure you didn't hit your head?"

He leads me into a makeshift office, with an old table in one corner, and chairs on either side. The walls are dark in here too, which seems to be the theme of the house, but most are covered in schedules, posters, and health and safety notices similar to the ones we have at my work.

Mason guides me into a chair and sets his things down. He instructs me to hold the icepack in place while he pulls another chair around to prop my foot up on.

"You hang out there for a second, and I'll just grab some paperwork. Necessary evil, I'm afraid."

I silently curse Peter as I try to get comfortable. This is not how I wanted tonight to go at all.

Mason flips through a folder and makes a surprised humming noise, uncapping his pen with his teeth. "Well, look at that. You've popped my cherry."

"Pardon?"

"First incident form of the haunt." He points to the number in the corner of the form. "001."

"Well, I'd be honoured if I weren't so annoyed. I've been looking forward to tonight for months."

"Really?"

His expression is endearing, and I hope he's better at scaring than first aid. All I'm getting right now are excited puppy vibes.

"Are you kidding me? Halloween is my favourite holiday. I've waited my whole life for a look inside this house, and it's already over. This is officially the worst date I've ever been on."

He sets another chair down in front of me and takes a seat, leaning in to rest his palm on my ankle. It's warm and weighty, and his fingers curl around me. We both look down at where his thumb strokes a patch of my skin, though he doesn't seem to realise he's doing it at first.

"I'll make sure you get free tickets so you can visit again," he says, pulling away and putting pen to paper. "What's your name?"

"Jenna Laing." I spell it out for him, knowing how often people miss the *'I'*.

"Date of birth?"

"September 13th, 1995."

"Are you serious? Mine is the 12th, but I'm two years older. Happy birthday for last month."

This man has no business being this cute with fake blood on his face. With blue eyes and messy hair, he's one of those people who smiles with his entire face, so you feel like the sun is shining right on you. Even with the gruesome effects, I can't look away, though I'd love to see what he looks like without his makeup, too.

He fires through the questions about my address and contact information, then slips a pocket watch from his waistcoat and notes down the time.

"Can you tell me what happened in as much detail as possible? I'd love to make sure nothing like this happens again."

He nods along, scribbling down the relevant details as I recount the events of the past thirty minutes.

"I can't believe your date ran off and left you alone in a haunted house."

I can't contain the snort that escapes me.

"It's fine. I don't think we were a good match, anyway. I'm a big horror girlie. It takes a lot to scare me, and he was trembling before we even set foot inside."

"What a pussy," he mutters, tapping his pen against the side of the clipboard.

"I don't like that," I tell him, and his gaze snaps up to mine.

I'm no stranger to calling people out on inappropriate or outdated language. I do it all the time at work. Just because our residents are old, it doesn't mean they can't learn to do better. And that applies to all of us.

"My apologies. That language was unprofessional. Forgive me."

"I'm not offended by your language, I'm offended by the sentiment. People use *'pussy'* like it's a weak thing. Everyone knows balls are way more sensitive, and pussies can take a good pounding any day of the week. And in this case, my date was one hundred percent testicle."

His eyebrows inch higher and higher, and I smile sweetly, quite content with my paraphrased little rant.

"Well, thank you for calling me out on it. I will remove that word from my lexicon."

A laugh bursts out of me, and I shake my head. "Oh, no. You can definitely still say pussy in other appropriate contexts."

"And, uh, what are the appropriate contexts?" he asks.

The air stills as his eyes linger on mine, challenging me to elaborate. My pulse rises, but there's no way on earth I'm looking away first.

"Like in the bedroom."

"Dirty talk?"

"Sure," I shrug.

Mason inhales deeply, his gaze dipping to my mouth. He sets his clipboard down and leans back against the desk, arms folded across his chest, those rolled-up sleeves straining against corded forearms.

"Care to give me an example?"

Damn, this man is a good flirt, but so am I, when given the opportunity.

"You just used lexicon in a sentence without batting an eyelid. I'm pretty sure you could come up with something."

"Like if I said, I'm gonna die if I don't taste your pussy in the next thirty seconds?" he asks without missing a beat. "Would that be appropriate? Contextually speaking."

My jaw drops. His eyes flick down to the hem of my skirt, and heat floods my core. Between the ice on my skin and the gravelly way *'pussy'* sounds coming from his mouth, I'm more than a little flustered.

I swallow hard while he waits for my answer.

"Yes. That would be an appropriate thing to say. Contextually speaking."

"Good to know."

The tension that hangs between us threatens to suck all the air from the room. His eyes are still on the spot between my legs, and when his tongue sneaks out to brush against the corner of his mouth, my thighs squeeze together. He notices, and his jaw ticks in response.

Beneath the underwear I vaguely hoped Peter might peel off me, I can feel my core throbbing. If he keeps this up, they'll be so damp I'll be peeling them off myself later. I wonder if I could orgasm just from the way he looks at me.

In something of a trance, he tilts his head to one side and—

Oh my God, can he see up my skirt?

The length is borderline indecent, especially when I'm sitting down, but I've never cared much for what people think about how I dress. Until now. My fingers curl around the hem, though I'm torn between pulling it down or lifting it up. Either way, it's enough to snap him out of it. He blinks rapidly, clearing his throat as he reaches for his clipboard, knocking it to the floor.

Sheets of paper spill loose, and he kneels before me to gather them up, once last sideways glance at my legs before forcing himself to look away.

He stands, composing himself with the clipboard held low over his groin, and it gives me a thrill to think we might have a similar effect on one another.

"I don't like that your date ran out on you, Jenna. Or that you need to leave here alone."

"It's cool, I'll call my—" I stop myself before I say '*dad*.' "A taxi."

"I have an alternative suggestion," he says playfully.

Even with an injury, I'm so horny right now I think I'd do literally anything this man told me to.

"If you're not too uncomfortable, you can come hang out in the bar for a few hours. I'll fix you a drink, find somewhere to prop your leg up, and I'll give you a ride home when we're finished."

Your shoulders would make a great place for my legs, I think.

"I beg your pardon?" he says, his jaw open in surprise.

Do not tell me I said that out loud.

"What?"

"Did you say something about my shoulders?"

Oh shit. This man really is messing with my head.

"Soldier!" I scramble to recover. "I think I can be a brave soldier. That's what I said. And I could murder a drink."

8

Jenna

This is the best first date I've ever been on, and technically speaking it's not even a date.

I have a great seat at the bar, my leg propped is up on a cushion, and every second Mason isn't fixing drinks, he spends flirting with me. At least, it feels like flirting.

I keep catching him looking at my legs, and every time it makes my heart race. His eyes coast a little higher each time until I'm certain he's not just checking on the wellbeing of my knee. Nobody has ever really looked at me this way, certainly not Peter, and I like it a lot.

Every ten minutes I watch a new group launch themselves through the door while escaping whoever terrorised them on the other side. I love seeing their panicked faces slip into relief when they realise they're in a safe place at last.

The room hums with nervous energy, and the people-watching is unmatched. Some can't stop laughing, some are on the verge of tears, and a few look like they might throw up.

Mason beckons them over to the bar and hands out *'I survived the Miller Mansion'* stickers. He is charming as hell, and every minute I spend in his company makes me want to know more about him.

Who is he, and where has he been my whole life?

He has a knack for cocktails and flair. When anyone orders shots, he lines the glasses up on the flat side of his axe and pours them from a height, never spilling a drop. I watch their expressions change when he stretches his arm across the bar, holding the axe level with their faces and barking *'drink'* at them with his best snarl.

He introduces me to Lulu, a stunning woman whose character flirts outrageously with all her customers, playfully degrading men who look like they were seconds away from pissing their pants.

Now and then, Mason breaks into a bit with one of the other staff, pushing and shoving and tussling until a third steps in to break up their 'fight', but it always ends in more brawling.

When one guy pulls a fake gun from behind his back, Mason quickly wrestles him into a headlock, and it turns out I was right. The sight of the two of them tussling and grunting turns me on far more than it should.

I'd let him put me in a headlock. With his thighs, ideally.

Jesus, I need to get laid.

By closing time, I'm not even sad about missing out on the haunt. I've had a front-row seat for a show most of tonight's visitors would only see for as long as it takes to finish a drink.

When the last customer leaves, Mason asks Lulu to make sure the staff are okay, then escorts me to where his car is waiting at the back of the house.

It's a mild night, but a fine mist hangs in the air. With no lights on this side of the building, I can't see far. If we were still in the haunt, I'd be waiting for a wall of zombies to rush out of the darkness any second.

Mason is a lot quieter on the drive, which eats away at the confidence his company has been building all night. I felt so at home back there with him, but in the real world, I can't help but wonder if it was all an act. Perhaps what felt like flirting was just very thorough customer service. It wouldn't be the first time I've misread signs.

"You can just drop me off here," I tell him when he turns onto my street. My house is barely a three-minute drive, and I'm wishing I walked.

He stops the van, gets out, and darts around to the passenger side. He opens my door with a warm smile and holds out his hand.

"I'd prefer to walk you to your door and make sure you get inside safely. If that's okay with you?"

Oh, of course he's a gentleman, too.

I've had a long time to check Mason out tonight, but I can't put my finger on what's so attractive about him. I don't exactly have a type. When you live in a small town, and have a reputation like mine, beggars can't be choosers. Not that I'm desperate enough to beg, it's more that there isn't much choice in the first place.

After a couple of hours of ice and elevation, my knee is fine, but I play along, taking his hand and letting him wrap his arm around my shoulders. He cups my elbow, his grip reassuringly strong. No surprise with hands the size of his.

Mason is tall and slim, with a cute, boyish face that matches his excitable energy, but sometimes an aura of dominance washes over him, and it completely disarms me. Did I dream that thing he said about dying if he didn't get to eat pussy? I cannot figure this man out.

He follows my lead, and I walk far slower than necessary up the short driveway to my house. We're almost at the door when I hear footsteps behind us, and two little furballs fly past our feet and up the front step.

"Hiya, sweetheart, was beginning to wonder if you were staying out all night." Dad hurries past me to unlock the door. "Go on Dolly, get inside. Whitney, stop sniffing around."

Mason looks down at the Pomeranian spinning in circles at his feet, a confused look on his face. I step out of his hold, putting space between us while Dad eyes up his torn-up costume.

"What the fuck happened to you, lad? You get in a fight?"

"He's one of the haunt actors at the Miller house," I explain. "This is..."

I pause, remembering he's not in character anymore. I've spent several hours quietly swooning over this man, but I don't actually know anything about him.

"Sorry, I never asked your real name."

"Mason is my real name," he smiles.

"Mason?" Dad interrupts. "I thought your date's name was Peter?"

"It was. It's a long story."

Dad crosses his arms and glares at me until I elaborate, playing down my injury and leaving out the part where Mason curled his fingers into the back of my knee. And especially the dirty talk part, even though his words have not stopped circling in the back of my mind.

Mason looks back and forth between us. It's not the first time someone has misread our situation. My parents were twenty when I was born, and Dad still has all of his hair without a hint of grey.

"So *Dad*," I emphasise. "This is Mason. Mason, this is my father, Terry."

"Ah, your Dad," he sighs, holding out his hand. "Pleasure to meet you, Mr Laing, and happy to make sure she got home safe."

"Well, thank you for that. Now, are you coming in, or shall I give you five minutes for canoodling?" he laughs, turning serious as he points a finger at Mason. "Five minutes and not a second longer, you understand me?"

Mason stands tall and makes an awkward, strained noise. Dad closes the door, leaving us alone under the porch light. I am so mortified I want to disappear into the mist.

"He lives to embarrass me. Sorry."

"You live with your dad?" he asks, stepping further back. His tone is even and non-judgmental, but shame curdles beneath my skin. Thirty years old, and still living at home. What a catch.

"Both my parents," I correct him, as if that makes it any better. "And my brother. Well, he moved out for a bit, then he broke up with his boyfriend, so now he's back. I'm saving up for a deposit, but the housing market is out of control around here. You can't even buy a one-bedroom place unless you're loaded, which I'm not. And anyway, it's handy for work, so..."

Shut the fuck up, Jenna.

We've had a lot of short snippets of conversation tonight, and I think I did a half-decent job of playing it cool, but I was bound to overshare and screw it up at some point. He doesn't need to know this stuff. Mason is hot, and funny, and has an interesting job he's clearly very passionate about. Of course, he wouldn't actually be interested in me.

"What do you do for—"

I cut him off, reaching for the handle and stepping inside. "Thank you for driving me home. For the drink and the chat. And the icepack."

Once the door is closed, I lean back against it and finish the thought in silence.

And for making me feel more alive than I have in months.

9

Mason

A WEEK AND A bit later, I'm still replaying opening night. Specifically Jenna Laing, and the way she goaded me into dirty talk in my office.

And her lips.

And her hair.

And her gorgeous thighs.

I want to spread them apart, tear those fishnets wide open, and sink my teeth into her skin. Thought about that more than is healthy, to be honest.

Every night has run smoothly, and every night I've watched the door of the Tavern, hoping to see her walk through it.

Last Tuesday, I pulled her number from her first aid paperwork and called to follow up on her accident, as per protocol. She didn't answer, and I chickened out of leaving a voicemail, but I still can't get her off my mind.

The fact that I know where she lives is haunting me, but turning up on her doorstep doesn't feel appropriate. And anyway, contacting her for anything beyond work-related purposes is a breach of confidentiality guidelines. I'm trying to keep things professional, even if my thoughts about her are entirely unprofessional.

After a couple of hours in her company, something shifted when I walked her to her door, and our night ended before I could...

Honestly, I don't know what I had in mind. It's not like I have any free nights to take her out. Who knows how long I'll even be in town. Dating is not a distraction I need right now, but I know I would have kept talking on her doorstep all night. And I definitely would have been up for five minutes of canoodling if she'd let me kiss her.

Our first week has been great, but I'm a little stir-crazy spending all my time in the house. I guess that's bound to happen when you live where you work, so I'm forcing myself to walk down the hill into town to grab a coffee most mornings.

When I was planning the haunt, my research veered into the old market town of Crowmorne, and I learned the cobbled streets were once bustling with businesses. Half of them are now coffee shops, but that's great news for someone as caffeine dependent as me. I'm determined to try them all, and today's spot is *Happy Crow Coffee*, where I hope the drinks are neither made from, or served by crows.

I never figured out how the town got its name, but the locals sure love birds, and you can spot them in most shop windows. The bakery sells crow-nuts, there's a salon called *Hair We Crow*, and the community vegetable garden has a sign that says *'Crow Your Own'*. The puns are tenuous at best, but that's part of the charm.

The line is short, and the woman in front of me has dark hair pulled back in a high ponytail, and a figure that reminds me of Jenna's. She places her order, and when she makes her way to the other end of the counter, I catch sight of a long blonde streak hanging loose in her face.

Holy shit. It *is* Jenna.

She's in a world of her own, toe-tapping along with whatever she's listening to. I place my order, then lean into her eyeline and give her a little wave.

She glances over her shoulder, then back at me, before removing one earbud and staring at me blankly.

"Hi?"

"It's Mason. We met last week. At the Miller house?"

Her makeup is more natural than the last time I saw her, but those lips are just as full and pretty. I watch them open and close, pinch into a pout, then break into a smile as her eyes run the length of my body.

"How could I forget? You still have blood on your face."

She reaches for my cheek, then quickly pulls her hand back without touching me. I rub at the spot she's been looking at, though I'm sure it does nothing.

"It's the fake stuff. Occupational hazard, I'm afraid. Can never get it all off before I have to put it back on the next night. How are you? How's the knee?"

"It's fine." She lifts her foot, extending and retracting her leg to prove it. "Think I have your magic ice-pack to thank for that."

She's wearing dark green trousers with clean white trainers, and a grey zipped-up hoodie underneath her black leather jacket. It's a totally different look to the outfit I saw her in last week, but still cute as fuck.

I've had plenty of time to think about what I'd say when—*if*—I saw her again, but now I'm standing face to face with her, words fail me. The hold this woman has over me is unreal. I'm an actor, for fuck's sake. I'm never speechless, but I can't stop staring.

"Pumpkin spice latte," the barista calls out. Jenna takes it with a warm thank you.

"Well," she says awkwardly, her lips pinching together. "Nice to see you again."

"Do you have plans today?" I blurt out.

She looks down at her feet. "I'm heading to work."

"Can I walk you there?"

A passing interaction isn't going to cut it for me. I'll do anything to spend a little more time in her company.

Jenna stares up at me, a little crease forming between her brows. Her head tips one way, then the other, before she shrugs and her frown turns into a smile. "Sure. Why not?"

She heads for the door, and I bounce on my heels while waiting for my coffee, then almost knock a chair over in a hurry to catch up with her.

Late autumn sun warms the street, and she basks in it as she tucks her other earbud away.

She was gorgeous at night, but by day she's something else entirely. A little softer, but with plenty of clues to her personality, if you're looking for them, which I am.

A slick of black eyeliner. Dark red nails. A pin on her jacket of a skeleton reading a book. A pendant at the hollow of her throat that I mistake for a cross, but is actually a dagger.

No fishnets, unfortunately.

"You haven't been back to the house."

"Have you been watching out for me?"

"Maybe."

She takes a tentative sip of her latte to hide her smile. I'm coming on strong, but she has no idea how disappointing it is when every guest who walks through that door isn't her.

"I was hoping I'd run into you in better circumstances."

"I have tickets for Wednesday night, so you might see me then."

"Another date?"

Please say no.

"Friend from work."

"Hopefully, this one is braver than the last guy."

Jenna corrects me. "She is."

"*She*. Good."

"And why is that good?"

"I just mean I'm glad it's not a guy. Or, I don't know, maybe you're bi," I blurt out, then immediately panic. "That's fine if you are. Obviously. That's none of my business. I don't really know you, but I want to. Sorry, this is my third coffee. I haven't slept much lately. All those late nights are catching up with me, and then I just lie there staring at the ceiling thinking about new ways to scare people. For the haunt. Not because I'm a creep or anything. Work scares only from this guy."

I tap my chest with my thumb, then realise I'm running out of air. Jenna's hand covers my other one, pulling my cup away from my face.

"You sure that's only your third coffee?" Her warm smile grounds me. "And I thought I was an over-sharer."

This is not like me. Since when do I get stage fright or... whatever this is? Jenna looks bewildered, and it's ironic that my bumbling bullshit might freak her out more than anything I could pull off in the house.

I take a deep breath to compose myself. "I'm sorry, I... I was just really hoping I'd run into you."

"So you said."

"And I didn't want to scare you off again."

Her eyebrows knit together, and she stares at her coffee, swirling the cup through the air.

"You didn't. I was just a little overwhelmed by the whole evening. I didn't think you'd walk me to my door, and I get awkward when I'm nervous."

"Well, that's fantastic." My tone is far too enthusiastic. "We should start a support group or something. Same time next week? We can take turns seeing who can be the biggest weirdo. Not that you're weird or anything. I don't mean that. You seem great. I like your hair."

Through an amused snort, she mutters something that sounds like *'this fucking guy'*.

"Three coffees is definitely your limit, dude."

Oh, fuck no.

How did I blow this so fast? I don't want to be in *'dude'* territory or anything close to the friend zone with her.

Jenna rolls her eyes and strides off, calling back over her shoulder. "Are you walking me to work or not?"

I run to catch up, and she asks about my week, but only a few minutes later she stops outside a big house, set back from the road. I've walked past a few times, but never really paid attention. The *'Crowmorne Heights'* sign is blue and white, and the smaller text below tells me this is a residential home.

Jenna twists to face me, her shoulders pulling back as she squares off with me. "This is me."

The street is familiar, and looking around, it takes a second to realise the house where I dropped her off last week is right next door.

"You work *here*?"

"Yep. I'm a Senior Care Manager." She hugs her arms around herself and stares at the floor. Suddenly, her green trousers make much more sense. "I know it's pretty pathetic, still living with my parents, working right next door, but they own this place, and I've worked here since I was sixteen. Can't imagine doing anything else now."

I've been wondering what a woman like Jenna Laing does for a living, but I wouldn't have picked this. Everything I learn about her only fuels my curiosity.

"It's not pathetic," I tell her, nudging the toe of her shoe with mine. "That's very noble work. And people would kill for a commute this short."

"That's why I grab a drink from *Happy Crow* most mornings. Walk a loop around town, and try to mentally separate home from work."

"That's what I've been doing. The days kind of blur into one when you sleep at the office." I raise my cup for emphasis.

"Wait, you're living at the Miller house?" Jenna frowns while taking another sip of hers.

"Well, yeah. It's my house."

She nearly chokes, grabbing my arm to steady herself. "Hold on a second. Are you telling me you're Old Man Miller's illegitimate son?"

"Not a son," I clarify. "Distant nephew and only living descendant, apparently. He never had children, but his sister was my great-great-aunt, I think. I'd never even heard of him or Crowmorne until I got a phone call from an executor who'd been trying to track me down for two years."

She drums her fingers on the lid of her cup. "Fuck me. I did *not* think my brother would be right about that theory."

"Your brother had theories about me?"

"About the house, sure. Everyone in town had one. You know, I've been obsessed with that house since I was a little girl. I want to know everything about it, but—"

"I'll give you a tour," I interrupt.

Her face lights up, but then she looks back at the building. "I need to go before the residents start curtain-twitching."

She saunters up the path, but I'm not leaving until she's out of sight. Halfway up, she turns to call back to me.

"Hey Mason Miller, why are you so nervous to talk to me?"

"Have you seen yourself, Jenna Laing?"

She bursts out laughing, shaking her head as she scans her work pass to enter the building.

I catch myself just before I trip off the edge of the pavement, but I know I'd willingly throw myself into traffic to hear her laugh like that again.

10

Jenna

Mason is waiting outside *Happy Crow Coffee* the next morning, with a takeout cup in each hand.

It was wishful thinking to hope nobody had noticed me talking to him outside work yesterday. Elsie, Roland, and Joyce love spying on people from the windows, but they love gossiping even more, and I was bombarded with questions about Mason all day.

Obviously, I didn't answer them, but they raised plenty of my own. I'd assumed some events company had hired him, but now I know he owns the Miller house, I'm even more intrigued.

I'm not a morning person, and he caught me off guard yesterday, but I was still replaying our conversation as I fell asleep.

It's colder today, but he looks cute as hell in black jeans and a green turtleneck underneath a black wool coat. Very dark academia. A bright smile spreads across his face when he spots me and hands one cup over.

"Pumpkin spice latte, right? If you prefer something else, I'll go back in."

"Are you stalking me, Mason? That's only hot in dark romance, not in real life."

His laugh is genuine, but dies abruptly. "God no. I just wanted to see you again, and you mentioned you get coffee here before work and I..."

For a man who seems so self-assured when I watched him banter with customers at the haunt, he sure gets flustered easily. It's kind of charming.

His nose wrinkles, and he rubs the back of his neck. "I've overstepped, haven't I?"

"It's fine," I tell him, and sighs in relief.

"Still not scaring you off?"

"Takes a lot more than a free coffee to scare me." I let that first sweet sip warm my mouth, grateful for the extra cinnamon they add here. "And pumpkin spice is correct. I've tried every place in town, and this one makes the best ones."

"Good intel. I'll keep that in mind."

"Are you walking me to work again?"

"Would that be okay?"

"Sure."

An older couple walks towards us, and we step aside to make space on the narrow pavement. Mason loops his arm around my shoulder without thinking. My gut instinct is to pull away before anyone sees, but I fight against it. Who cares what people think?

Knowing he saved me a few minutes by ordering my drink, I walk more slowly and answer his questions about life in Crowmorne.

Every shop we pass has a crow in a costume in the window, part of a town-wide treasure trail for the local kids. Some have made more effort than others, though it's a little too family-friendly for my tastes.

"You guys go big on the spooky stuff here," he says, and my coffee goes down the wrong way.

"You'd think with a name like Crowmorne, everyone would be a spooky fucker, but for years I've been the only creep in town. This is all the Miller effect. You've been very good for business."

I tell him how the extra attention on the house has brought in more money, how pleased our pubs and restaurants are to have more customers during the week.

"You must know everyone," he says.

The noise I make is deeply sarcastic. "Pretty much, and that's not a good thing."

"How so?"

"It's hard to explain," I deflect, not wanting to dig up years of trauma about not fitting in here. "Where did you grow up?"

"South London," he tells me. "My mum died when I was three, so it was just me and my dad. Then he died too, not long after my nineteenth birthday. Mum had cancer, Dad had his demons, drank his way to his own cancer."

"Oh, I'm so sorry. That must have been awful."

Many of our residents have had cancer over the years, but no matter how much you work with it, it doesn't make it any less shit.

"It's okay," he shrugs, clearly not wanting to get into his baggage either. "I've been bouncing around London ever since, taking acting jobs, some improv stuff. The small-town, everyone-knows-everyone vibe isn't something I've ever really experienced."

"Well, you're the talk of the town here."

"Am I really?"

"Oh yes, and not just local businesses. My residents want to know all about you. A few asked if I'd take them up to the house for a visit, but I wouldn't want to be responsible for sending them to an early grave. Speaking of which, I should probably say goodbye here."

I duck out from underneath his arm before we get to my house, keeping my back to my neighbour's hedge. I don't need Mum or Dad spotting us either.

"Why?"

"Your fan club will be waiting to get paparazzi shots through the window." He laughs, his eyebrows shooting up. "Don't let it go to your head. They're a feral bunch, and we don't get new men in Crowmorne very often."

"Are you still talking to the guy from last week?"

"Wimpy Peter?" I laugh. "Literally haven't heard from him."

"So, back on the apps?"

Oh my God, just ask me out already.

I keep the thought to myself, but I really wish he would.

"I don't think so. The dating pool is small, and the men around here are much too young, much too old, or extremely—"

"Vanilla?" he interrupts, surprising me with his boldness.

"I'm not vanilla shaming," I tell him. "If that's your kink, it's fine."

"But it's not yours, is it?"

No, it definitely isn't.

There isn't time to get into that conversation right now, but his casual observation has my heart racing. Mason's eyes dip to my mouth, then back up again. We're clearly both thinking about something dirty.

"I know you need to go to work, but I wanted to ask you something."

Ask me out.

Ask me out.

Ask me out.

"I have your number from your first aid paperwork, but I can't use it for non-work purposes without your permission."

A thin squeak escapes my lips as I fight the biggest smile. "And what would those non-work purposes be?"

He taps my cup with his, stepping closer, crowding my body with his. "Maybe I'm not content with ten minutes of flirting over morning coffee."

"Oh, we're flirting, are we?"

"Well, I wouldn't want to assume your intentions, but I most definitely am."

"Then yes, you can use my number."

"Great," he says, stepping back. "And I'll see you tomorrow night in the Tavern."

11

Jenna

Mum leaps three feet in the air, then buries her face against my back, pushing me away from two haunt actors intent on showing us their collection of dead pets.

I'd be inclined to stop and chat about them if Mum wasn't crushing the bones in my hand. She screams in my ear when another actor leaps out in front of us, dangling some sort of rodent. She shoves me so hard we almost tumble to the floor, but I catch myself on the door handle and twist it open.

There's never any way of knowing whether you're headed for safety or worse horrors, but when we burst through it we find ourselves in the Tavern. It's a stark change from what we've just been through, bustling with people calming their nerves with a drink.

"Is it over?" Mum says, her hands and face pressed to a wall like it's the thing that will save her. "Please tell me it's over."

I'm briefly disappointed, until Mason catches my eye from his spot behind the bar. His whole face lights up, and I feel mine do the same.

"Yeah, Mum. It's over."

"Thank God you know all about intimate hygiene care for old women, I think I'm going to pee my pants."

I pull my focus away to check on her, fixing my skirt and my hair while my back is turned. Who knows what state I'm in after her manhandling me all night.

"You're not old," I tell her.

She is a scaredy-cat, though, and I knew she'd be the perfect companion for my second visit. These things are always better when you go with someone who thinks it's all real. Their fear and adrenaline feed mine, even if the setting isn't doing much for me.

That's not the case in the Miller house though. Every room was different from the last, and I found myself getting more and more invested in the story as the family made us play their spooky games.

I'm about to turn around when something pulls me backwards, and I look down to see the head of Mason's axe hooked over my shoulder.

"Miss Laing," he sing-songs in character, close to my ear. "How wonderful of you to visit us again. And I see you've brought your friend from work."

His voice makes the hair on the back of my neck stand on end, but not because I'm afraid. I duck free of his hold and try to keep my composure as I gaze up at him. He's as hot in costume as I remember, which isn't helping me play it cool.

"Friend from work?" Mum scoffs. "I'm her mum."

"Mason, this is Amanda. Mum, this is Mason." I wave back and forth between them, and he offers her his hand. "Mum is also my boss, so *technically* still a friend from work."

She shakes it firmly. "Please call me Mandy. So you're the famous Mason Miller, are you?"

He swings his axe up over his shoulder and turns to me, his surprised expression the opposite of my embarrassed one. "I don't know, am I famous?"

I have no idea what Mum is talking about. We're close, but not confessing our crushes close, and we literally haven't spoken about him.

"The one from all the canoodling on the doorstep, according to her father."

"Jesus," I groan. "There was no canoodling."

"Well, not yet anyway," Mason retorts with a wink.

My jaw drops, and Mum elbows me in the ribs before I can hide it.

"So, you survived the Miller mansion. Did you enjoy yourselves?" he asks, and I'm grateful for the change in subject.

"Hated it," Mum tells him bluntly. "Nearly peed myself. My daughter is the Halloween fan in our house, but she didn't get it from me. I'm a total wuss."

"Ah yes, your daughter is a very bold woman indeed," he says, pressing his tongue into his cheek. "And gorgeous, which she definitely got from you, Mandy."

He's not wrong. Mum is undeniably gorgeous, and I've spent most of my life watching people flirt with her. We have similar faces, and just like people sometimes mistake Dad for my partner, they often think Mum and I are sisters. Except she's glamorous, and confident, and makes friends wherever she goes, and I'm... well, not built that way.

I used to wonder if she'd have preferred a daughter who is more like her, but beyond her dislike of some of my childhood hobbies, she's never put any pressure on me to look, or act, or dress a certain way.

After I grew out of the teenage phase of hating everyone and everything, we've been much closer, and even if we're not at work, I really enjoy spending time with her. She has plenty of her own friends, but sometimes we do things just the two of us, and I appreciate those nights the most. Not everyone is so lucky in the parent department.

"Will you stay for a drink?" Mason asks. "I'll fix you something that'll really rattle your demons."

I want to tell him we'd love to, but I'm not about to ditch my own mother to stare at a barman, no matter how cute he is. And I'd much prefer to see him alone, anyway.

Thankfully, she answers before I get the chance. "I need to get home and hug my dogs and my husband before the nightmares kick in. In that order."

Mason gives her an understanding nod, stepping back into character.

"Well, I hope you'll grace us with your presence again soon, ladies. Be sure to tell your friends to visit us... and tell your enemies twice."

We weave our way through the crowd, and as we step out into the cold night air, I glance back, thrilled to find him watching me leave. He blows me a kiss with that same little wave he gave me the first night, and really I hope it won't be long until I see him again.

12

Mason

MASON: Sorry we didn't get to chat more last night.

JENNA: I'm sorry, my mum is so embarrassing.

MASON: You're very cute when you're embarrassed.

MASON: Would you like to come for a tour of the house on Saturday around noon?

JENNA: I thought you wanted my number for non-work purposes?

MASON: I do. This is strictly unprofessional.

13

Mason

Jenna arrives right on time, buzzing the rusty old intercom at the main gates.

I oiled them a few weeks ago, but I can still hear them creaking apart as I watch from the window. As soon as the gap is wide enough, she slips inside and hurries up the driveway.

It's a mild day, but the leaves that cling to the trees are a riot of autumn reds and golds. In a dark skirt, and tight orange sweater, Jenna fits right in. Her legs are bare, but her lips are painted dark, and I can't help but imagine them wrapped around my cock. Adjusting the front of my jeans, I bolt down the stairs, opening the door just before she rings the bell. At one time, there'd have been a member of staff to greet visitors, but I'm glad it's just me now.

"Pumpkin spice latte?" she says, handing over a cup. "I actually don't know your order."

"It's perfect, although I wasn't really a fan until I started copying your order."

Her smile widens, those cute cheeks turning pink. "You're never beating those stalker accusations, Miller."

"Truly, it's all been a ruse to get you here alone." That, and I wanted to know what her mouth tasted like. "Dare you enter my lair?"

"Oh, I dare," she laughs, pushing me aside. "I can't believe I'm getting to see this place in daylight. You know, when I was little, I used to ask if I could have my birthday party here?"

"That's adorable."

The noise she makes is part snort, part squeak. "Nobody thought it was adorable. I was a weird little creep. Other kids went to Disneyland, I wanted to play with ghosts in the spooky old house up the hill."

"All weird little creeps are welcome here. You're in good company."

I close the door, cutting us off from the outside world. We're still operating with old bulbs and whatever light seeps through the windows that haven't been cleaned in years. There are over one hundred of them, and a specialist company quoted me thousands, so the job dropped right to the bottom of the list.

On her previous visits, Jenna would have moved through the building on our schedule, but now she takes her time to look around, studying the ceiling and lightly stroking the intricate details of the wooden panelling.

"So you wanted to talk to me about something?" she says. I can hear the curiosity in her voice, with a hint of trepidation underneath.

"I did."

"Well, I'm here," she says, taking a sip of her coffee. "And I'm all ears."

"Follow me."

Haunt guests get led into the East wing, but today I want to show Jenna the place where I made all of this happen. I open a door on the opposite side of the hall, but when I motion for her to head through, she freezes.

"What's wrong?" I ask.

"I've never been on this side of the house."

"Well, you're a very special guest, remember?"

That earns me one of her gorgeous smiles, and with another tip of my head, she follows.

The first room we step into would once have been used to welcome visitors, but like many of the rooms, everything is covered in dust sheets.

"How very Dexter of you," Jenna says, taking it all in.

"I swear it was like this when I arrived. I promise I won't murder you."

"Dexter only kills bad guys, and I'm a very good girl, so I think I'm safe."

My head snaps in her direction, only to find her looking up at me. She throws me a wink, and I'm tempted to put her on her knees right here and get her to prove it.

This is how it feels to be around her. Ever since she twirled for me, I've had the overwhelming urge to tell her what to do. To take control of her body, shatter her into so many pieces that when I put her back together, she'll never be the same again. I want her to feel things she's never felt before, to fuck her into the deepest sleep of her life. Want her to wake up with a lingering ache from all the places I've grabbed and pinched and stretched her.

Want to give her a night she'll look back on years from now and feel hot at the memory. And I think, desperately hope, she wants that too.

I fold my arms across my chest. She tilts her head, drawing me into another staring contest as we both refuse to look away. I could stand here flirting with her all day, but I don't want things to go any further until we've had a proper conversation about it.

"Come on, we still have a way to go."

I lead her through the grand ballroom that stretches the full depth of the house, with windows to the front and tall doors that open out to the patio at the back. There's a history here that I haven't even begun to unfold, but I want to eventually. If the peeling walls could talk, I bet they'd have some amazing stories to tell.

Through the next door is another sitting room, with more wrapped furniture and a huge open fireplace. Jenna follows close behind me.

"It's like a time capsule."

"I don't think the old man used this part of the house at all. When I arrived, it seemed like he'd only been using the kitchen, bedroom, and bathroom for a long time. Other rooms were closed off and untouched for years."

"It's a big house for one person. I hope he wasn't lonely."

"Yeah, it's kind of creepy being here on your own. Especially at night after everyone leaves, and it's just me in my room. Lot of random creaks in old houses."

"Can I see your room?" She bites her lip, something I've noticed she does when she says something bold, then tries to hide it.

"Eventually. But first, you need to see the library."

I push open the double doors, delighted with the sound she makes when we step inside. Every wall is lined with books, floor to ceiling, with rolling ladders on the lower level and a staircase in the corner to reach a balcony that circles the room for access to the upper levels.

It's my favourite room in the house. The first time I came in here, I sat for hours, just taking it all in.

Most of the books are old and degrading, with that gorgeous musty smell people go nuts for. There were several desks in here, which made me wonder if this was a place for study at one point. There's nothing modern, and no soft furnishings, so it's not much of a reading room by modern standards, but I've made good use of it, anyway.

Jenna hovers in the doorway, her hand over her mouth.

"What's wrong?"

"Nothing," she says, her gaze bouncing in all directions. "This is incredible. All these years, and I had no idea what it was like inside."

I watch her explore at her own pace. She runs her fingertips along the spines, then leans in to take a deep sniff. Her satisfied sigh is heaven to witness. She likes it too.

"Do you want to see the original haunt plans?"

"I'd love to."

I guide her to where I lined the desks up in a long row in the middle of the room, and the roll of paper spread out on top. It's taped in parts and covered in scribbles, but this is where I spent weeks running up and down stairs, drawing maps and planning the haunt route.

The mansion is almost two houses, one enveloped by the other, with the main family rooms all connected by hidden doors and hallways designed to keep staff out of sight. Every detail of the experience came to life here, and by the time I'd invited a few friends up from London to test it out with me, I knew I was onto a winner.

Jenna traces one fingertip through my blueprints, and when she bends to look more closely, her skirt lifts a little at the back.

The urge to step closer behind her and bend her until her face presses into the desk is unbearable. I shove my fists in my pockets instead and keep my distance.

"This is incredible," she whispers, and my heart swells with pride. "The Ritual. That's my favourite room, I think."

"Really?"

"Oh my gosh, yes. It's terrifying." She presses her hand to her chest. "All those hooded figures just staring at you, not knowing which ones will move. Do you change it up each night?"

"We do."

"That's smart. Mum bolted, but I looked every one of those fuckers in the face, even though my heart was pounding. They got a genuine scream out of me when they finally tried to grab me."

It's subtle, the way her body language changes when she talks about being scared. For most people, the enjoyment of a haunt comes from the relief. It's like catching your breath after being on a rollercoaster, the chemical rush of euphoria that floods our systems once the frightening part is over.

But not Jenna Laing. She leans into the scare and stays in the moment.

In every room, she plays along with the characters, embracing the roleplay rather than trying to rush through and avoid them. After her visit, I heard several of the actors talk about how fun she was to interact with.

"So you inherit a mansion. Why turn it into a haunt?"

"It's a good way to make money fast. I've worked a few Halloween events in the past, so I figured I could give it a go. Spent a few weeks designing the rooms, and here we are."

"You make it sound so easy."

It might *sound* easy, but I drained the little savings I had to get up and running. Luck comes and goes in the blink of an eye. I know that better than anyone, but I didn't invite Jenna here to trauma dump on her.

"It's a gamble. I'm hoping it pays off."

"Why not sell it?"

I can't help but laugh, because that's what the lawyer, and pretty much all of my friends, told me to do when I heard the news. "That would be the smart thing to do. After taxes and all the legal fees I inherited, I'd still have a lot left over—"

"Oh, just a few million, I'm sure. How on earth would you cope?" Jenna prods me gently in the stomach. In a flash, I grab her wrist and keep her hand there, pressing it flat against me. She looks down at it, but doesn't pull away.

"Right? I could travel, buy a flat in London and stop living in grubby house shares, start a business." The list of possibilities is endless, but none of them would make me happier than making this place a home.

Though I was technically an adult when my dad died, his loss quickly showed me I knew fuck all about being a grown-up. In the years since, I've had too many addresses to count, and not a lot of stability. Friends have come and gone as quickly as jobs, and I've never entertained thoughts of the future, because what's the point when you don't know how much future you've got.

"Something made you stay."

"Yeah, I mean, look around. I didn't feel like I could just sign it away to someone else. I had someone from an auction house visit to value the furniture, but I don't want to sell things off if I can help it. These things were here long before me. They deserve to stay."

She hums softly and lets go of me, pressing the same palm to her chest.

"You're a good custodian. I've seen a lot of people move their family members into our care and dump their furniture. Those things hold memories, and not everyone gets it."

"That's really sad. I figured I could live here for a year and then make a more permanent decision about the future of the estate. There's a lot of land, mostly woodland and overgrown meadows, but there's potential, I'm sure of it."

She goes back to the maps and drawings, her face lighting up as she reads through my scrappy notes.

"You know the house is legendary around here? People have been curious about it for decades. You could open it up for tours all year round."

"Everyone knows the real draw of those places is tea and scones. It would take a lot of work to fit an industrial kitchen, add toilets, make everything properly accessible. I'm just one person, with limited cash flow, but I need to come up with something or I'll end up having to sell it anyway."

"That would be a shame."

"Why's that?"

She drops a hand on my shoulder and squeezes softly. "Who'll keep me company on my morning coffee walks?"

14

Jenna

Mason's plans are incredible, and I'm so grateful he's taken the time to show them to me. I follow the sketched route through the rooms again, this time paying special attention to his notes on where the actors enter and leave. If I hadn't already visited, I'd be spoiling the experience for myself, but this is a level of detail most people don't get to see.

Next to the floor-plans, he's drawn the Miller family tree, and I trace them back through the centuries.

"The old family bible has marriage records in it, so I managed to piece a bit of history together starting with..." He leans in, tapping the paper right next to my finger. "Archibald Miller."

I stare down at our hands, willing him to shift just a little to the left. "You made them the story. That's clever."

"I mapped out the names and dates, but there wasn't much else to go on. The family kept to themselves, but I knew there'd be a lot of intrigue, so it made sense to base the story on them. They probably weren't evil monsters, but the truth is often scarier than fiction, right?"

"I'm just glad you didn't go with zombies," I laugh.

"Not a fan?" He hooks his pinky over mine, brushing it gently.

"It's overdone. They're so predictable in their movements, their pacing. You can always tell when they're going to switch things up and lunge for you. Also not a fan of anything that relies on making disabilities and disfigurement seem scary. That never sits right with me."

"Me neither. So what would really terrify you?" he asks, and I twist to face him. He's closer than I realised, and I rest my bum against the edge of the desk.

"Your double bluffs are great. When I walk into a new room, I'm immediately checking behind me, because I know that's where people will jump out from. You have the guy under the sofa, and those actors hidden in the hallways. They're fantastic because nobody expects them to be there."

"We built a fake wall, and they hide behind the paintings. Everyone wants a part there."

"How did you recruit your actors?" My biggest worry about visiting was that I might see familiar faces, family of residents, or people from school I never talk to.

"A few are friends from London who catch the train up. Most are local volunteers, or students from the drama school in Bramwell. People do it because they love scaring, or it's good acting experience."

"I had no idea so many people in Crowmorne were into Halloween."

"Guess you're not the only creep in town after all." His movements are subtle, but I feel the heat of him as he shifts closer. "I feel like you should have applied."

"I'd rather be on the receiving end of the scaring," I tell him.

He reaches between us to twist a strand of my hair around his finger, and I swallow hard.

"You like it when things are out of your control."

It's not a question, it's a statement of fact. He's always watching carefully, making observations that go beyond the words coming out of my mouth. He did it when he said I wasn't vanilla, honing straight in on my preferences from just a little flirting.

His close attention means he's learning a lot about me, but I still know very little about him.

"Can I ask you something?"

"Anything," he says, still playing with my hair.

"Most people would assume that scare actors are sick fucks who love to mess with people. But you seem like a genuinely nice guy."

"That's not a question."

"I guess I'm asking, are you a nice guy or a sick fuck?"

He traces his finger down the column of my throat.

"Heaven forbid a man wants to be both."

He nudges the toe of my boot with his shoe, and I shift to make room for him to step between my legs. This close, I have to tip my head back to look up at him.

Fuck, he's so gorgeous. A girl could lose her grip on reality for a man like Mason. Maybe I already am.

His thighs press against the inside of mine, his hands sweeping my hair back over my shoulders. He drags them down the length of my arms, resting them on top of where I'm gripping the edge of the desk. This is the most contact we've had since he stroked the back of my knee, but I want more.

"Scaring people in real life makes you an asshole, but scaring people for a job is..." He falters, searching for the best way to finish his sentence. "Unique. I've always loved acting and improv. Creating work that makes people feel something is a rush. That feeling just happens to be fear in this scenario."

"Do you get off on it?" I ask, desperate to know if his brain is wired the same way mine is.

"It gives me a rush, but I'm not working every night with a hard-on, if that's what you're asking."

Well, if I wasn't thinking about his dick before, I definitely am now.

"Hey, Jenna. My eyes are up here."

Can you blame a girl for glancing downwards?

"What about you?" he asks. "Does it turn you on? Being scared."

My brain short-circuits for a moment, and I feel light-headed. His hands wrap around my wrists, his fingertips pressing into the thin skin where my pulse is thrumming.

"Answer me."

"Yes," I sigh, swaying a little.

"Can you explain it to me? What it feels like."

I've never really thought about it in much depth. I may not have a lot of physical experience, but mentally I've taken myself to a lot of places. In the fantasies I revisit most often, I'm not in charge. The partner in my head decides for me, takes what they want, uses me.

In that moment, I don't want to think. I just want to exist as a body, a vessel made for pleasure. A plaything.

Mason looms over me, watching closely, but giving me space to get my thoughts together. I've never had a conversation like this. Never been with anyone who's taken much of an interest in what I like, let alone encouraged me to dig into the *why*.

"My life is predictable," I eventually manage to say. "I go to work, I do the same tasks on repeat, I come home, eat dinner with my parents, watch a bit of TV, and go to bed with a book. It's a good life, but it's normal. Boring."

"You wish things were unpredictable?"

"Yeah, sometimes," I huff out, practically panting with the need to relieve the pressure building between my legs. Mason's smile doubles in size. "What's that smile about?"

"This smile?" he says, pointing at his face. "Oh nothing. Just thinking about some new ideas for the house. For you."

"What kind of ideas?"

"I'm figuring out the details."

He still has my hands pinned to the desk, but I sit up straight, pressing my chest against his in defiance. He breathes deeply, his mouth so close to mine it almost feels like he's drinking my soul.

"I swear to God, Mason, if I find out you're actually a ghost and this is some sort of sexy Casper situation, I'll be so pissed off."

Would I still want to fuck him if he *was* a ghost? Probably. He could visit me in my dreams, and I'd wake up covered in ectoplasm and—

Jesus, I really am a creep.

He drags a line across my cheek with the tip of his nose, and my eyes drift closed. "I promise you I'm real."

"Then prove it."

I hear him break into a smile, then feel him blow a hot breath against my neck. "Does that feel real?"

I feel it sparking everywhere. "No, that's definitely not human."

"What about this?" He grazes the shell of my ear with his teeth, and it turns me into a puddle.

"I can't feel a thing," I whisper. "Maybe you should try kissing me. I bet that would work."

"You know, I would have kissed you outside your house if your dad hadn't interrupted us."

A frustrated moan catches in the back of my throat. The tension is unbearable, and I need him to do *anything* to break it. "He's not here now. What are you waiting for?"

15

Jenna

Mason pulls me away from the desk, slipping his hand into mine as he drags me out of the library.

"Where are we going?" I ask.

"You'll see."

His legs are so much longer than mine, and he strides ahead while I struggle to keep up. Room after room passes in a blur, and I lose track of where we are in the house as he leads me into the servants' corridor, up a set of stairs, back in the opposite direction, then into a tiny room.

He slams the door behind us, pressing me up against it with the full weight of his body. Our mouths find each other instantly in the dark. His hands thread through the hair at the nape of my neck, yanking to tip my head back. My lips part, and that first taste of his tongue is electric and salty and my new addiction.

We are a blur of hands reaching out, tongues seeking more, bodies pushing and pulling. Time loses all meaning as he devours me. He presses his knee between my legs, and I moan into his mouth, then again when he snags my lip between his teeth and tugs hard.

I whimper, hoping he leaves a mark, but the noise makes him pull back. His ragged breath fills my mouth as we fight for the same air. I'm about to kiss him again when he reaches for a switch, and an old Edison bulb flickers to life above us. Even in the low orange glow I can tell his pupils are blown, and his lips are full and slick from where I've sucked at them. He dips his head to inspect mine with a sweep of his thumb. I can't resist lapping at it, and I'm rewarded with a deep groan. We're as greedy as each other, it seems.

He drops his forehead to mine and cages me in, one palm flat above my head. The other hand grips my waist, keeping me pinned against the door. It's hypnotic, the way he takes up all the space around me, making me feel small and safe in his presence. I briefly wonder if I've hit my head and am now living in some fictional reality. Real men aren't like this.

"What is this place?" I ask, peeking behind him at the rows of empty shelves.

"Old laundry storage, I think. Ever since I found it, I felt like it would be a perfect spot for hiding away and making out."

He tucks my hair behind my ears and cups my face, holding me close enough to check how I'm feeling.

"And who exactly are we hiding from?" I ask.

"The ghosts, obviously."

"Ah, of course. Ghosts famously hate laundry."

"All those years being mistaken for bedsheets. Who can blame them?" He shrugs one shoulder, and I slip my hands behind his neck.

"Do you think we should do it again? Since we're so safe in here." I tip up and kiss the smile right off his face.

This one is softer, and I let him dictate the pace. When he's done with my mouth, he trails his kisses down my throat, sucking softly at my neck.

Nobody has ever kissed me this way, like they can't get enough. He grips my hips, squeezing the softest parts of me, then palms my breast through my clothes. The pressure is everything, and still I need *more.* His thumbs slip underneath my sweater, and I want him everywhere.

I cling to his shoulders, and we keep going, grabbing at each other, until we hear distant voices. Mason groans and kisses me firmly before reluctantly pulling away.

"The haunt crew are here," he whispers.

I bury my face in his chest, hating what that means. We can't hide in a closet and make out all afternoon, as much as I'd love to.

Releasing my grip on his t-shirt, I reach for the fake scar that's now semi-permanent.

"You still have blood on you." I brush his cheek gently, then do the same with his mouth. "And now my lipstick too."

"Good." He sucks my thumb, and when my head thumps back against the wood, he wraps his other hand around my throat, cradling me there.

Dust motes drift through the air, probably hundreds of years old, but I can't think about that when he's looking at me like I'm his next meal.

"Do you have plans for Halloween?" he asks.

My head swims at the sudden shift in tone.

"Uh, scaring the kids on my street while they threaten to egg my house. Busiest night of the year for you, I assume?"

"We're fully booked, but that's our last night. The crew are heading to the *Sun and Stars* for a wrap party afterwards. I was hoping you could meet me once they're all gone."

"I'm sure I can be free," I shrug. I'm playing it cool. I will *definitely* be free. "What do you have in mind?"

"Like I said, I'm still figuring out all the details."

"And when will I get to find out these precious details?"

"Soon," he smiles, adjusting the hair around my face. "Can you come back tomorrow?"

16

Mason

We open earlier on Sundays, so there's no time to waste. I grab Jenna's hand and lead her through the start of the haunt, past the briefing area, and straight through Lady Miller's drawing room.

Even though the actors won't be on site for another hour, you can still feel their presence—or the presence of something—in these dusty old rooms.

I've never really believed in ghosts, though I've spent plenty of time in old London pubs and theatres, abandoned buildings and old film-sets for commercial shoots. You'd think if they were real, I'd have seen one by now, but this house has a way of making you feel like there's always something lurking around the corner.

When I first moved in, it was a little unsettling, and it took me a few days to get comfortable being here alone. Now the random creaks and noises don't bother me so much. Who am I to mess with any spirits who've been here since long before I was born?

We take a side door that's off limits to haunt guests, and head along the corridor to the office where I helped her with her knee. How is it possible that was only two weeks ago?

From the look on her face, I can tell she's disappointed.

"I've already been in here," she pouts.

"You'll see more of the house later. I want to run through a few things first."

I've got a million ideas for the unused rooms, but I need to narrow them down without giving too much away. For this to work, and for Jenna to get the most out of our time together, it has to be a night full of surprises.

I pull out the chair on the opposite side of my desk. "Take a seat."

Jenna sits with her back straight, hands folded neatly in her lap, and I wonder if she's more nervous than she's letting on. I only want to make her nervous when she's consented to it, which is exactly why this conversation is so important.

"Is this about these mysterious ideas you were hinting at?"

"Maybe," I shrug, sitting in my own chair.

"Mason," she whines, throwing her head back. "Just tell me already. I could barely sleep wondering what tricks you have up your sleeve."

Oh, I have so many tricks, but I'm having too much fun playing with her. I lean my elbows on the desk and rest my chin on my clasped hands.

"I have a proposition for you, but I want to make sure you know what you're agreeing to."

"And that is...?"

"I want to design a custom experience for you. Strictly one-on-one."

Her face twists through various expressions before landing on confused. "You want to haunt me alone?"

"Something like that. On Halloween night, you'll come up here, and we'll play a game. Think of it like Trick or Treat, the after-dark version."

She must blink a thousand times, her chest heaving as my words sink in. "Are you saying..."

I lean forward until my eyes are level with hers. There can be no mistaking my meaning here.

"I want to scare the fuck out of you, Jenna. And then I want to fuck the scared out of you."

Her jaw drops, and her eyes widen before her lips roll inward and her cheeks turn a pretty shade of pink. Oh, yes. She understands me just fine.

"Let me get this straight," she says, drumming her fingertips on her knees. "You're offering me a night of creepy sex in your creepy old house?"

"I never said the sex would be creepy," I laugh.

"It's kind of implied, isn't it?" she says, lowering her voice and cocking her head. "Mysterious stranger. Mysterious house. Mysterious sex plans. Don't worry, in case you hadn't noticed, I'm into creepy shit."

I had noticed, and I fucking love it.

"Then yes, that's what I'm offering. Creepy, mysterious, all of the above. If you're interested?"

She answers so fast it's actually hilarious. "I'm interested. You've got yourself a deal, Miller."

She stretches her hand across the table, and my face hurts from smiling so much. I swear my heart is going to beat right out of my chest if I'm not careful.

"We need to go over a few things first, then we can shake on it."

"What things?"

"Boundaries, limits, expectations. I'll never put you in danger. That's the number one thing I need you to know."

She leans in and pumps her eyebrows up and down. "What if I like a little danger?"

Looks like someone found their confidence after all. I knew she'd be the perfect person to play these games with.

"My job here is to make people *feel* like they're in danger, when really their safety is my priority."

Jenna slumps back in her chair, folding her arms across her chest. "Am I a *job* to you?"

"More like a side quest."

"Wow, you really know how to make a girl feel special." She tries to hide her smile by looking down and fiddling with the cuff of her sleeve, but I'm watching far too closely to miss it. "Why would you do this for me?"

"Customer satisfaction is important to me."

"You do this for all your customers?"

"No, Jenna. You're one of a kind. And honestly, totally unexpected. I never thought I'd meet anyone like you here."

Her eyes narrow, and she folds her arms across her chest. "What do you mean, *'like me'*? I'm not into that *'you're not like other girls'* bullshit men love to say."

I fucking hate that nobody's treated her right. "I'm sure there are other women like you, but I've yet to meet one as cute and sexy and fun to play with."

She laughs, and I'm grateful for the sound of it. What I'm proposing isn't exactly normal. There's no easy way to explain my vision, and every time I see her I'm terrified I'll say something that has her running out on me.

Opening my desk drawer, I lift out a clipboard with the paperwork I prepared this morning. "Shall we get started?"

"What is that?" she asks, scooting her chair closer to the desk.

"It's a quiz about kinks, so I can learn what you like, and what you don't like."

"Ooh, like a sexy medical." She flips her hair back, sits up straight, and shimmies her shoulders. "Okay, Doctor. I'm ready for you."

It bodes well that she snaps into a little roleplay so easily, and I can barely contain my excitement.

"Should I buy a white coat?"

"Oh God yes," she moans sarcastically. "That would really do it for me. Ask away."

Doctor kink, huh? Let's find out what else Miss Jenna Laing is into.

17

Mason

"Why don't you start by telling me about things you've enjoyed in the past? If you're comfortable?"

This is usually a good way to ease ourselves into the subject, but Jenna puffs out a harsh sigh and looks at her hands.

"Truthfully, Mason, I don't have a lot of experience, and I don't mind telling you that. You know, I've lived here my whole life, my closest friends are my residents, and I still live at home. Any relationships I've had have been the short-lived kind where I sneak them in and out without waking my parents."

"So you've never had a screaming orgasm?" I ask. Her eyes widen as she looks back up at me. "I'm sorry. That was too much."

"No, it wasn't. It's actually refreshing to talk to someone like this, but you're right. Being loud isn't an option."

"But you'd like it to be?"

She lifts one shoulder, feigning indifference. "I don't think I'd hate it. I can get pretty loud in my head, but they're just fantasies."

Fantasies I'm dying to make her reality.

"Tell me about them."

Most people need a little time to warm up to these discussions, and silence is a useful tool. The longer I let it stretch out between us, the deeper she'll get.

"What's in this for you?" she asks.

"I enjoy creating situations and experiences that make you feel good. This isn't about me." I wait to see if she understands what I'm saying.

"Are you some kind of pleasure dom or something?"

"Bingo."

"For real? I thought that was just fictional men."

The thrill I get from eliciting a reaction from people is difficult to describe. Watching our guests shriek, and scream, and laugh, and panic. The moment their fear drops into relief. People show you their rawest emotions in a haunted house. They can't hide them.

Scaring people doesn't arouse me at work, but it makes sense those feelings would carry into the bedroom. I've always been much more interested in a partner's pleasure than my own.

There's nothing like bringing someone to the edge of ecstasy and then ripping it away, or overstimulating them to the point of exhaustion. And when they think they can't handle any more, you push them until they prove to themselves that they can. It's been a while since I've had someone to play with like that, but watching Jenna get lost in my touch, my words, my actions...

Fuck. I'm getting hard just thinking about it.

I bet she would look so pretty with tears of pleasure running down her face.

"What if I'm not the right person for this?" she asks quietly. "For you?"

I want to reach out and touch her, to prove just how wrong she is.

"There hasn't been one single thing I've learned about you that I haven't liked, but I want to know everything. So, let's work through this list, and you can be totally honest with me. There are no right or wrong answers here. Are you ready?"

"Okay," she says, sighing heavily and stretching her neck from side to side. "This is fucking nuts, but okay."

"Do you have a safeword?" I ask, knowing that's the best place to get started.

"I like the traffic light system. Assume you're familiar?"

"Yes, but just to check, red means stop, yellow means slow down, green means keep going?"

"Correct."

"Good. We need to trust each other to respect those words. You can use them anytime you like. I'm not interested in hurting you, even if I enjoy the illusion of it. No matter what we do together, you always have the power, even if I make you feel powerless. Do you understand?"

"Yes."

She's cautious at first, but her answers confirm my suspicions about what she enjoys, and once Jenna opens up, there's no holding back. It's a crime that she hasn't had much opportunity to explore the things she's curious about, her deepest and darkest desires. Soon she's answering before I've even finished the question.

"Oh, just give me the clipboard."

Fired up and impatient, she snatches it from my hand, plucks a pen from the pot on my desk, and rushes through the rest of the questions. When she's finished, she pushes it back in my direction with a smug smile.

I glance down at the page where she's checked every 'yes' box. Shaking my head, I pull the paper free, tear it in half, and shove it in my pocket.

Jenna gasps, then pouts. "But I said yes!"

"Nobody is into *everything*. If you tell me you have no limits, you're giving me permission for things I don't think you've really thought about. You're really okay if I feed you dog food until you throw up?"

She screws up her nose. "Ew, no. I don't want that. Was that on there?"

"Not specifically, but that's why we're talking about this stuff. Your curiosity is a gift that you need to handle with care. We can't do *anything* if you don't take this seriously."

I slide open the bottom drawer of my desk and lift out the spare copy I printed for this exact reason.

"You knew I'd mess up?"

"No, but I had a feeling you might have a bratty side. Are you wearing underwear right now?"

Her head snaps back, mouth forming a pretty O-shape. "What did you say?"

"Underneath your skirt, which is very cute, by the way, are you wearing anything?"

She toys with the hem. "Uh, yes."

"Stand up and take them off."

I lean back in my chair and wait, watching her swallow hard. Her eyes flit from side to side, and I can practically see her brain sparring with itself. Part of her wants to defy me, I can tell, and the other part wants to do exactly as she's told.

It's a test, but she clears her throat, stands up and reaches underneath her skirt. I watch her hook her thumbs into the elastic and push her underwear slowly down her thighs. She steps out of them and presents them to me, dangling on the tip of one finger.

I'd love to shove them in my other pocket and keep them, maybe wrap them around my dick when I crawl into bed later, but I shake my head.

"Put them in your mouth."

18

Jenna

If there was a movie of my life, this is the record-scratch, freeze-frame *'yep, that's me. You're probably wondering how I got here'* moment.

Standing in the Miller house, stripping out of my underwear and shoving them in my mouth simply because a man I barely know told me to.

And I've never been more turned on.

Mason's entire demeanour shifts as he watches me follow his orders. His jaw ticks and his eyes darken. He feels bigger somehow, and the air in the room thickens when he tilts his head to one side, stares at my skirt, and adjusts the front of his jeans.

He tugs off his sweater and rakes his fingers through his hair. Guess I'm not the only one feeling the heat in this room.

"Sit back down, and we'll start over. Nod your head if the answer is yes, shake if it's no. You want to say something, you raise your hand and wait until I tell you to speak. Understood?"

I nod, my chest heaving as I try to control my breathing through my nose. I'm not a small woman, so neither are my underwear. Even balled up tight, they don't leave a lot of room for air.

"These questions are important to me because *you* are important to me. Think of it as a risk assessment. I want to create something special for you, but I don't want to make assumptions, and I'm not taking any chances with your body or your mind. I need you to know deep down that you're safe, even if you don't feel like it when we're in a scene together."

I don't love being scolded—or maybe I do in this case—but Mason is right. His proposal is so wildly unexpected, I'm swept up in the thrill of anticipation and not thinking clearly. With the way my core is throbbing, I'd say yes to anything, but I appreciate a man who understands consent and wants to focus on my pleasure. That certainly hasn't been the case with some of the lazy losers I've dated in the past.

He starts over, repeating the questions designed to assess my comfort levels with various acts, positions, dynamics. Just like before, my answers are mostly yes, but since I can't interrupt, he forces me to slow down.

"Anal?"

Slowly, I raise my hand, and when he gives me permission to speak, I remove the fabric stuffed in my mouth.

"You may speak," he says.

"I've never..." I stumble over my words and take a deep breath. "I've never done anything there before. But I'd like to try."

"It's not something we would rush into," he says matter-of-factly, scribbling a note in the margin of his paper. "We'd need time to take it slow and prepare, so maybe that's something for another night. I'm sure we can find a middle ground. Now put your panties back in your mouth."

I do it without hesitation, and when he calls me *'good girl'*, a thin whine seeps out of me.

"Toys?" he continues, running through a list of types. I nod along with all of them. "I want you to know that everything I use will be new and sanitised. Hygiene is important to me. I'll use condoms, but I haven't been with anyone since my last test results were clear. Anything I should know about there?"

I shake my head. It's been a couple of years since my last test, but I haven't been with anyone since then, either. Thank God I didn't break that dry spell with Peter.

Mason keeps going with questions about blindfolds, and restraints, and temperature play. In the long, drawn-out pauses between, my mind runs riot trying to imagine what he's plotting with this information. I want to know everything, but it's also exciting that I don't.

The thought of walking into this house, knowing full well I'm about to get railed by a man who creates scare haunts for a living, is just...

Honestly, what the fuck is happening to me?

When he asks about fisting, my focus flicks down to his hands. They're big, and I've never tried it, but I'm curious about the sensation of being stretched and full.

That's the beauty of Mason's plan. We'd have plenty of time to play, and zero interruptions. Like anal, I'm sure we could work our way up to it, but my head is swimming with the reality.

I shake my head, and he doesn't bat an eyelid.

He lists off names he might call me.

Whore. Nod.

Bitch. Nod.

Slut. Nod.

When his questions turn to edging and overstimulation, I feel like I might come from the lack of air and constantly clenching around nothing.

When I masturbate, I often force myself to push through the sensitivity. In the dark quiet of my room, I imagine my partner growling in my ear, demanding I give them more. Orgasm denial is the opposite experience, but the allure is still the same. Someone else taking control of my body and my pleasure, focusing solely on me, all give and no take. The thought is unbearably sexy.

I cross my legs, rubbing my thighs together, hoping for a little relief. My eyes flutter closed when I find it, but it's not enough. Shifting my legs the other way doesn't help, either.

"Jenna, are you okay? Do you need a break?"

My moan comes out all muffled, but when I look back at him, he licks his lips and smirks. He knows this is driving me crazy, and I think he enjoys watching me squirm.

"Exhibitionism," he continues. "Are you interested in having an audience?"

I think about it for a while before raising my hand and waiting for his permission to speak. I can't tell what's wetter, the panties in my mouth, or the back of my skirt where I must be soaking it.

"I like the fantasy, but in reality, I'd get too self-conscious and worry about what people think of my body. So not for this."

"That's good. And anyway, I want you all for myself. You're fucking hot, by the way. For the avoidance of doubt."

He says it like it's the most casual statement in the world, not an open declaration of his feelings towards me. Never has a man been so open and direct before, and I feel it throughout my entire body.

"I take it that's the same for group activities?"

I nod, and put the gag back in without being prompted. Mason keeps going, guiding me through the rest of his questions, elaborating on a few.

When he's finished, he talks me through his own limits and boundaries. Hearing him describe the things he enjoys is a rush, and though it's clear he'll be in charge, it's reassuring to know what makes him feel good too. Consent works both ways, and I don't want to be second-guessing anything in the moment.

He drops his pen into the holder and puts the clipboard, along with all my answers, in his desk drawer. I watch as he locks it, then pockets the key.

Since we're done, I assume it's okay to take the gag out, but I liked being called a good girl earlier, so I wait for his permission.

The seconds feel like hours when he's staring at me from across the desk, blatantly exploring my body with his gaze. I didn't think I could feel any warmer than I already am, but sweat is beading underneath my top, and I don't know whether I want to cool it down or turn up the heat.

I haven't always been kind to myself when it comes to my appearance, though things have been better in recent years. The older I get, the less I give a shit about what people think. I am who I am, and I'm not interested in changing to please others.

In school, I often felt like I was the only one getting bullied, but looking back, I'm sure everyone had it rough at some point. I was an easy target for immature kids, mostly because my parents ran a retirement home.

People would say I had thirty grandads, and somehow that meant I was inbred. Or that I stank of piss, which is offensive both to me and to the residents.

The few classmates who ever came to my house would run screaming at the sight of the skull collection in my bedroom, sparking rumours that spread so rapidly the police turned up to make sure I wasn't the infamous and elusive Crowmorne Cat Killer. There'd been a lot of suspects that year, though most people eventually accepted it was a fox.

When I hit puberty before everyone in my year, the joke was that I was stealing food from grannies to grow tits. And people wonder why I prefer the company of older people? Kids are pricks, teenagers are worse, and I can only hope that biology lessons have advanced in the last fifteen years because that's obviously not how digestion works.

And then there are men. The ones I've been with haven't always been kind either. Subtle comments that landed like a brick. Comparing me with their exes. A frustrating lack of attention or care in the bedroom, and certainly nothing that's ever resembled worship.

But Mason? Mason obviously cares about my pleasure, and he's still looking at me like I'm a fucking prize.

"You can take those out now," he says eventually.

I consider putting them back on, but I drop them on his desk instead. He presses his tongue into the side of his cheek, and I can tell he wasn't expecting it.

"So what's the verdict?" I ask.

"I think you're my dream girl, Jenna Laing."

19

Jenna

On the outside, I try to act cool. This is no big deal. A perfectly normal Sunday afternoon, discussing my deepest sexual fantasies with a man who frightens people for a job. Who among us *hasn't* been in that situation?

On the inside? I'm kicking and screaming and blushing all over while I wait for him to make the next move.

"Stand up," he says, and I do it before he's even finished speaking. He beckons me closer, and I round the desk with as much grace as I can manage under the circumstances. He spreads his knees wide and taps the top of his thigh with his fingertips.

"Sit."

He's so fucking cool about all of this. It's ridiculous how much I want to follow his orders, but nervous laughter bubbles up inside me, and I hesitate.

"I don't know if the chair will take the weight of both of us."

"Don't be a brat."

"I'm not," I protest, even though the accusation makes me want to double down and see where a little bratty behaviour might lead. "It looks pretty old."

He wiggles his hips to prove how sturdy it is, and fair play to him, it doesn't even creak.

"Do you trust me, Jenna?"

That question makes me laugh too. "Honestly? I barely know you."

"You will soon enough," he smiles. "I know I'm asking for a lot here."

His palm wraps around the side of my thigh, and I make an embarrassing squeak at the contact with my bare skin. He slips it behind me, squeezing to pull me closer.

"I'll never put you in any danger, remember? Not ever."

I believe him. Nobody makes you fill out a kink quiz unless they really care about your wellbeing. I might not know much about him, but I know I'm safe here.

His head tips further back so he can hold eye contact, drawing me deeper under his spell. His voice is hypnotic, his touch makes me woozy. His hand slides higher, lightly stroking the curve of my ass. The other hand mirrors the movement, until both are full of my cheeks, fingertips pressing gently into my flesh.

"It aches, right?"

"So much," I nod.

"I know it does. I saw you squirming while you answered my questions. Don't you need a little relief?"

Words fail me. I can only manage a whimper.

"Then ride my fucking thigh."

His rougher tone shocks me, and I grip his shoulders when he tugs me forward and down onto him. The pressure of him, flat and hard against my core is incredible, and I groan at the sensation.

"There we go," he smirks, skating his fingertips up and down my skin. "Isn't that better?"

I breathe deeply, trying to compose myself, but he presses onto his toes, pushing harder up against me. I shift my weight, desperate for relief from the ache he's been building inside me. My clit drags against his jeans, and the friction sends sparks shooting through my limbs. I move to kiss him, but he ducks away and spreads his arms out wide.

"Nope. I'm just here for the show," he says with a teasing laugh. "Grind harder."

My eyes squeeze shut, but when I open them, Mason is still watching me closely, his face lit up like he just got everything on his Christmas list and more. He bounces his knee, my hips buck, and I grip the back of his neck while he watches me lose my shit.

"Oh, fuck," I moan.

It's embarrassing how hard I ride his thigh, but I don't care. I've needed this since he kissed me in the laundry closet yesterday, and the orgasms I managed alone barely took the edge off. There's no stopping me now. I'm going to come on this man's leg before he's ever properly touched me. That's how much power he has over me.

My thighs grip around his so I don't lose my balance. Heat floods through me, the pressure building and building until—

A knock on the office door interrupts us.

"Hey boss!" someone calls from the other side. "We have crow-nuts backstage."

"*Nooo*—" I whine, and Mason grabs my head with both hands, one palm clamped over my mouth.

"I'll be right there," he calls back, a smug grin on his face. "Playtime's over. Time to get up."

I hold his shoulders for support while he helps me stand up. He tugs my skirt down from where it's ridden up and guides me to the door.

"God, you were so close, weren't you? Such a shame." His mocking tone only makes me want him more.

He opens the door and peers into the corridor, checking the coast is clear

"Do you, er, think you could find your way out?" he asks, scrubbing at his jaw. "I need to run upstairs and change before I see anyone."

I glance down at the wet spot I've left on his jeans, and my hands fly to my mouth. "Fuck, I'm so sorry."

"Don't be." He loops an arm around my waist and pulls me closer. "I loved seeing you get that heated and, you know, it *is* my fault you're not wearing underwear."

"They were soaked before I even took them off."

He gasps, then flicks the hem of my skirt up a little. Silently, I will him to go higher, to take a proper look at what we both know he'll find underneath.

He smoothes the sides of my hair and plants a soft kiss on my forehead. "Will you text me and let me know you get home safe?"

The way this man switches it up between soft and dominant is giving me whiplash.

"I'm sure I'll manage, but if I get into an accident and paramedics see me half-naked, I'll ask them to put me out of my misery right there. And I will absolutely haunt you from the afterlife."

"Haunted by a ghost with a hot, bare cunt? I think I've seen that porno."

Now it's my turn to be shocked, though even hearing him say that word does wicked things to me.

For Mason, that thought seems to trigger another. "Oh hey, on Halloween night, can you do something for me?"

"Depends on the something," I tease, though at this point I think I'd crawl through glass for Mason Miller.

"Can you wear your fishnets again? The ones from the night we met."

I fucking knew it.

Every time I've replayed it, I think about the way he looked at my legs, how he slipped his fingers behind my knee and toyed with the material.

"Of course. I want this to be good for you, too."

He kisses my cheek and whispers in my ear when we hear more voices in the distance.

"Trust me, if you're having a good time, I'm having a great time. You don't have to worry about me."

Ah yes, the whole pleasure dom thing. Did not have that on my bingo card this year, or this lifetime, to be fair.

"Okay, well..." I trail off. I've got nowhere to be, but I know he needs to start work. "Happy haunting, I guess."

"Happy fingering yourself into oblivion the second you get home."

Mason throws me a wink as he darts in the opposite direction, and it's a miracle I make it out of his house in one piece. Mine is thankfully empty when I get home, and I ride my vibrator until the battery dies, wondering what the fuck I've just agreed to.

20

Mason

It took weeks to prepare for the Miller haunt, but I've only had four days to prepare for my night with Jenna.

There's a lot less to think about when you're only planning to scare one person, but I'm a perfectionist, and I'm not slacking off where her pleasure is concerned. Every day, a new package has arrived, but then even more ideas have come to me.

I've read and re-read her kink quiz so many times, and still can't believe how perfect she is. She's so open-minded, and curious, and playful. My dick has barely gone down since I watched her grind herself into my thigh the other day. I wanted to touch her, wanted to get my hands on all of those perfect curves, but it's better that I didn't. I need to prove to her that she's in control when she's in this house, even if she's handing it over to me.

She'll be worth the wait, I have no doubt about it.

Despite covering so much in our discussion, there were still things I forgot to check. Thankfully, I have her number, and her permission to use it. While the crew file in for our final briefing, I unlock my phone and revisit our messages from the past few days.

MASON: Do you have any allergies?

JENNA: None.

MASON: Any phobias? Are you good with small spaces?

JENNA: No and yes.

MASON: Clowns?

JENNA: If you fuck me dressed as a clown, it better be from behind with a bag over my head.

JENNA: What the hell are you planning?

MASON: You'll see. Count your days.

No more counting. Day zero is finally here.

Every member of the team has gathered backstage before we open the doors for the last haunt of the season.

"You doing okay, boss?" Lulu asks. "You seem distracted."

If I seem distracted, it's because I am. There's no time left to go back and check the rooms I've set up for Jenna, even though I know I have everything covered.

Clarissa wraps an arm around my shoulder and gives me a big squeeze. "I can't believe it's Halloween already," she says, her real voice nowhere near as proper as her character's. "I'm really going to miss playing Lady Miller."

"You've done such a good job," I croak, surprised by the lump in my throat. "Okay, okay. Huddle in, team."

Their chatter dies off, and I run through the same briefing I have every other night, with the additional news of the money I've put behind the bar in the *Sun and Stars* for their wrap party.

The room fills with cheers and applause, and I'm sure there are happy faces beneath their gruesome make-up.

"Can we come back next year?" Sammy asks, and everyone pipes up with similar sentiments.

"How about you let me sleep for a week, then I'll run the numbers and think about it. One last time, what's our motto?"

"Scaring is caring!" they scream back at me, the loudest they've been.

We hug and shake hands, and when they file out I head for my spot at the top of the stairs.

On opening night, I did it out of curiosity. The second night, I did it in case Jenna came back. Now it's part of my act, but it's also a chance to take it all in and reflect on how far we've come.

Six months ago, my life was at a standstill. No purpose, no job, not a lot of hope. I have no idea what life will be like in another six months, but even if I can't keep the house, this haunt will always be something I look back on with pride.

In rehearsals, I liked to be everywhere all at once, checking on the cast, making sure they were sticking to the story I'd created and giving it their all.

Truthfully, they could run this night without me. Whether they're old timers or this is their first experience of scare acting, they've been an incredible team. Whatever the future holds, they'll always be part of the Miller family history.

The first doorbell rings out through the halls. Beneath me, Ron gives his head a shake and shifts into Jessop mode, shuffling forward to open the door.

"Come on in then," he grunts. "If ya dare."

The group tiptoe in around him, shrieking when he slams it shut. I lean against the railing and dangle my axe over the edge, swinging it back and forth.

One more haunt, and then the real fun can begin.

21

Jenna

It is beyond ridiculous to be sneaking out at my age, but how am I supposed to explain leaving the house this close to midnight in the sluttiest outfit I own?

"Oh, don't mind me, Mum and Dad. I'm just off to get my guts rearranged in a haunted house with a guy who's into kinky roleplay. Don't wait up!"

Yeah, I don't think so.

Halloween is the one day of the year I can fully embrace my desire to dress like a creepy witchy woman, and easily blend in with the crowds, but this is pushing the limits of public decency for both the living and the dead.

My underwear is minuscule, my cleavage would turn a priest, and my skirt is impossible to bend over in, even though that's exactly why I chose it.

And, per Mason's request, I'm wearing fishnet tights that offer zero warmth against the chill in the air.

I'd considered wearing just a bra underneath my jacket, but threw a pink cashmere sweater over the top at the last minute. Hopefully, Mason will enjoy peeling it off me later.

My skin is prickling with goosebumps, but that's nothing new. I've been a bundle of excited, nervous energy all week, and counting down the hours until I finished work.

Our residents welcome any excuse for a celebration, so I set up the cinema room for an afternoon screening of *The Exorcist*, with spooky-themed cupcakes as a treat. Popcorn tossed with a few fake spiders would have been fun, but it's not great for people who have difficulties eating or end up with bits stuck in their false teeth. And I can think of at least one resident who would have eaten the spider anyway.

Some people say they don't make scary movies like they used to, but a few people fell asleep in the first ten minutes, and the rest enjoyed spoiling every scene before the big reveal.

They lost all interest when Joyce regaled us with a story about going to see it at *'the flicks'* when it originally came out, and how the boy she was *'courting'* at the time ran out screaming. I told her he sounded like he might have been a relative of my disastrous date, and we had a good giggle about it.

These are some of my favourite days at work, when our activities unlock old memories, and I get to hear all about the lives they lived before they moved into our care.

The dating scene might look a lot different now, but from the way she describes her youth, the butterflies are timeless, and mine are running wild.

After work, Dad and I changed into our outfits; him a vampire and me a witch. The trick or treaters started early and finished late, and we took turns to leap out from behind the bushes and frighten the kids before filling their buckets with sweets.

Marcus and I loved trick or treating when we were kids, but I always took it too literally. He'd ask for a treat, and I always asked to be tricked. None of the houses we visited ever prepared an actual scare, and the parents of my classmates would look at me like I'd brought dogshit to their doorstep. I'd skulk home disappointed nobody had cast a spell on me, or snuck a frog into my bag of goodies.

I read all the spooky stories I could find, and believed them, too. The Halloweens of my teens were spent trying to summon ghosts with a homemade ouija board, and hanging stick figures in the woods. If magic exists, I don't seem to possess any, but I still lean into the spirit of the holiday.

When I arrive, the gates are locked, and I jump when they creak open before I reach the intercom. They're too old to have automatic sensors, so I know Mason must be watching me, but from where?

The haunt team has cleared out quickly, and the long walk up to the house is deathly quiet. Gone is the ticketing booth and queuing system, the lights are off, and the crows in the trees might still be there, but it's hard to tell. There's no moon tonight, and my eyes play tricks on me in the pitch dark.

The front door is ajar, but unlike when I've been here in the daylight hours, Mason isn't here to greet me. I slip inside and push it closed behind me. It's not much lighter in here, and I immediately look around to see where he might appear from.

Haunt music is still playing from the speakers he has hidden around the place, but it stops suddenly, and a shiver zips down my spine when a voice crackles over them instead. Low, slow, and a little bit flirty. It's not Mason's natural voice, but it's undeniably him.

"Welcome to the Miller Mansion, Miss Laing. Your host for the evening has been eagerly awaiting your arrival."

"That makes two of us," I mutter to nobody. The voice continues, and I stand tall, listening intently.

"Mr Miller has chosen you personally for one unforgettable night of surprises, but there are a few things you should remember as a guest in his home. Number one, expect the unexpected. Number two, you can run, but you can't hide. And number three, if you scream, only the ghosts will hear you. Are you ready to find out if you will survive the Miller mansion?"

It's the same question Jessop asks when guests arrive at the haunt, before he tells them about the history of the family and sends them on their way.

"Oh, Jenna," Mason sing-songs. "I asked you a question."

I thought this was a recording, and hadn't realised I'm supposed to answer out loud.

"Yes," I answer, turning in circles, still no clearer on where he actually is. "I'm ready."

"Good girl," he says. "Now find the key, and find your freak."

The sound cuts out, leaving me in silence but for a few distant creaks. With the way my heart is pounding, I can't tell if I want to find the key quickly, or drag this out. I look around the entrance hall for clues, but there's nothing waiting anywhere obvious.

It's not on the table, or the stairs, or hanging from any of the doorknobs. I feel my way around the tops of doorframes, desperation building in my chest.

Finally, I find it on a hook behind one of the dark velvet drapes. A large old key tied to a paper label that says *'The Doctor'*.

I flip it over to find rough lines scribbled on the back, and it takes me a minute to understand it's a map. Once I get orientated, I head through the doors at the back of the room, and follow his directions into part of the house I haven't visited before.

Like most of the rooms, dustsheets cover everything, but there's no time to take it all in when I'm on a mission to find him.

The line stops at the end of a hallway, but there are three doors, and I don't know which to choose, until I spot a notecard pinned to the one which reads:

Please wait inside. Your physician will be with you shortly.

My hand trembles as I reach for the doorknob. I've never been this nervous or excited in my whole life. Shaking my arms out, I psych myself up, force a few deep breaths, and head inside.

22

Jenna

Like the rest of the house, the room is dark, except for an examination table in the middle of the room, lit from above by a tall angled lamp. Unlike the rest of the house, it smells faintly of bleach. Silent and clinical.

My haunt senses kick in, and I scan the shadowy spaces to see where he might be lurking, ready to leap out and... well, who the fuck knows what he's going to do here. I have no idea if he's planned for jump scares, mind-games, psychological terror, or all three.

When there's no sign of him, I approach the table slowly and examine the scene he's set up. The table is a serious piece of equipment. Sturdy, with a padded top, and two supports for the patient's legs.

My legs.

A terrifying thought worms through my curiosity. It's exactly like the ones I've seen in my doctor's office, and I'm sure they're expensive. What if this table's been in the house all this time and they used to perform experiments here?

I've read plenty of books about body snatchers and the horrible history of medical research. Everyone knows these old houses have secrets. I might be into freaky shit, but I'm not a trauma tourist. I don't want to fuck on a hospital bed where people were actually murdered.

A loud knock at the door jolts me to attention.

"Come in?" I answer, my voice cracking a little.

Mason enters, striding into the light with a warm smile on his face.

"Good evening, Miss Laing. I'm Doctor Miller. Sorry to keep you waiting."

He extends his hand, and I shake it while his gaze drags from my head to my toes. He doesn't try to be discreet about it, but I don't care because I love the way Mason looks at me. While he breathes deeply, I use the time to stare back.

What I said about having a doctor's kink was a playful joke, but he's clearly taken it to heart. In his pristine white lab coat, he'd fit right in at any hospital, and suddenly I can't think of anything hotter than being on the receiving end of this man's bedside manner.

"I'll be conducting your examination today," he says, releasing my hand and pulling a rolling trolley out from the shadows.

He picks up the clipboard on top, revealing a neat row of what are clearly medical implements, but it's too dark to identify them. They vary in size, and one glistens as he adjusts the angle of the lamp. It looks like a scalpel, and my throat tightens as I try to recall the questions he made me answer.

Did I agree to knife play? I can't remember now. I was too fucking horny standing there with my underwear in my mouth.

"And what examination will that be?" I ask, faking a level of confidence that definitely isn't in the room with us.

"It's nothing to worry about. Just a few preliminary checks to ensure your suitability and preparedness for this evening's events. Please allow me to take your jacket."

I turn to let him slip it off my shoulders. He breaks character and tosses it somewhere behind him. I guess I won't be needing it here.

When I turn back, he's impossibly close, forcing me to look up at him.

I've been desperate to kiss him again, have barely stopped thinking about our time in the laundry closet. I'm certain he's going to make me wait while I play his games, but that doesn't mean I can't push his buttons, too.

I drag a finger down the lapel of his coat and tug on his tie. "Do I get a hospital gown?"

My outfit is cute, but I want to get in on the roleplay, too. He bites back a smile, his hands brushing my hair over my shoulders.

"What you're wearing is perfect," he says in his real voice, before clearing his throat and adopting a more authoritative tone. "Whenever you're ready, you can sit up on the bench for me."

Mason has a knack for making me want to follow his orders and rebel against them at the same time. I like the way his mind works, and the way it makes me want to get into battle with him. In the seconds it takes me to decide what to do, he grips my hips and pushes me back against the hard edge, and a high-pitched whine escapes my mouth.

I boost myself up onto the end, and wait to be told how to position myself. Never have I found being legs spread in one of these beds sexy, but never have I had a doctor who looks like Mason, either.

"Where did you get a table with stirrups?" I ask, swinging my legs back and forth.

He snorts. "This is a doctor's office, Miss Laing. What did you expect?"

"But nobody died here, right?"

Mason rests his hand on my knee. I stop my swinging, but he leaves it there and leans in close.

"It's a stage prop," he whispers. His tongue darts out to tease the shell of my ear, and his shaky breath warms my skin. My eyes flutter closed and my body melts towards him.

He hooks the tip of one finger beneath one strand of my tights and lifts it away from my thigh. I hold my breath, waiting for whatever comes next. When he lets go, it snaps against my skin, and my eyes fly open. It doesn't hurt, but it still shocks me, and Mason smiles warmly.

"Nobody died here." His smile drops and he tilts his head, staring me down with a look I can't place. "Not yet, anyway."

A fresh wave of fear floods my system. I don't know where these games begin and where they end, but I definitely don't want this to be my last night on earth. Was sneaking out without telling anyone where I was going a huge mistake? My phone is in my jacket pocket, and I can't even see it with the overhead light so close to my face.

Mason is completely in control of my safety right now, and if I've walked into a deathtrap just because he made me horny, I really am the stupidest person alive.

He must sense my panic when he walks his fingers up the top of my thigh, tickling me lightly as he pushes the hem of my skirt higher.

"Please lay back and relax for me," he says sweetly. "This won't take long."

I do as I'm told, and rest my hands on my stomach, fingers clasped together just as I would during a real medical appointment.

Mason pats the pockets of his coat and pulls an old dictaphone from one of them, clicking it on.

"I'll be recording my observations throughout your examination. Please try your best to be quiet, and when I ask you questions, you can respond with a simple yes or no. Understood?"

Oh, how he loves to push me into this quiet, compliant role. I nod, and he holds eye contact while he presses record and speaks into the dictaphone.

"Patient is Miss Jenna Laing. L-A-I-N-G. Thirty years old. White British, brown hair, brown eyes, average height, exceptional figure."

My face flushes at my body being commented on in such an indirect manner. I'm not sure anyone has ever described me as exceptional. He circles the bed as he continues, his face hidden behind the light.

"Though she is a perfectly functional member of society, Miss Laing presents as an extremely depraved individual. Her most frequent symptoms include an unbearable ache in her lower stomach area and frequent overwhelming thoughts of a disturbing sexual nature. Patient masturbates multiple times a day but still seeks further stimulation."

My throat burns. Guess we're ticking the humiliation kink off early, but he's not wrong. I've lost count of how many times I've made myself come thinking about tonight.

"We are working on the hypothesis that the patient is a cock-hungry whore. Recommended treatment is a rapid course of exposure therapy that we hope will cure her of this terrible sickness."

I stifle a laugh with my palm, pretty sure that his brand of therapy will have the opposite effect. Mason flicks through a few pages on the clipboard.

"Our records show you recently suffered a knee injury, Miss Laing. Are there any ongoing issues there?"

"None at all."

"Any discomfort while kneeling?"

How he's keeping a straight face is beyond me. We both know why I'm here, and we both know why he's asking.

"I'm more than happy to kneel," I tell him, arching my back and pushing my chest a little higher. He definitely notices.

"That's wonderful news, but I'd like to check you have a full range of motion, just to be sure. Can you stay on your back and lift your leg up for me?"

I comply with my lips pinched together, and he cups my ankle.

"Pull your knee back, then extend it."

"And the other one." We repeat the action, and he hums his approval. "Now pull both knees up to your chest and keep them there."

I curl inward, wrapping my arms around the backs of my legs, and crossing my ankles. Mason stands at the foot of the table, reaches up to adjust the angle of the light, and shines it directly up my skirt.

He grunts out a low curse, and that deep noise is so raw, so real, there's a very strong chance it will be in every fantasy I get off to for the rest of my life.

A long time passes. I can't be sure how much, but I just lie there, staring up at nothing while he studies me. He presses the dictaphone again.

"Patient has full range of motion in both legs. For the record, she is wearing black lace underwear and black fishnet tights at the request of her practitioner. She responds to instructions without hesitation or discomfort. Very promising."

I bask in his praise, watching as he hooks his fingertips into my tights, twisting the material around them.

"Why did you tell me to wear fishnets?" I ask. I know exactly why, I just want to hear him say it.

"Because they turn me on, and you look fucking delicious in them."

"Oh," I gasp, then giggle. "That doesn't seem like a very professional thing to say, Doctor."

"Seems like you're impossible to be professional around."

He spreads his fingers beneath the strands, dragging his nails down my sensitive skin when he releases me.

When he moves to the head of the bed, I try to follow his face, but it disappears into the darkness above me. He taps my knee, and I put my legs back down, waiting for whatever comes next.

I hear him rummaging in his pockets, then the unmistakable sound of gloves snapping on.

"Open your mouth for me and say *'ahh'*."

23

Jenna

Based on literally every medical interaction I've ever had, I expect him to use a flat tongue depressor, but he surprises me by sliding two fingers into my mouth, sweeping them around the inside of my cheeks like a swab.

I want to be a good patient, but with the size of his hands, it's a struggle not to close my lips around them and suck. Mason keeps going, slipping right to the back of my throat.

"Swallow," he says.

My eyes water, and I focus on my breathing, determined not to choke.

"Gag reflex is minimal," he dictates. "Throat is well hydrated."

That much is obvious when he removes his fingers, slick with my saliva. He smears it across my face, squeezing my cheeks until my lips open. His fingers slip inside and hook behind my bottom teeth, pulling my jaw wider.

He drags his hand lower and wraps it around my throat, pressing his thumb and fingers into the sides. He studies his wrist, counting off my thrumming pulse. I'm so busy wishing he'd press a little harder it takes a while for me to notice he's not even wearing a watch.

"As expected, patient displays many of the common whore symptoms. Pulse rate is high, breath is rapid, pupils dilated. Investigations will continue."

Shifting to my side, he squeezes up and down the length of my arms, lifting one, then the other, and letting them drop.

"Any other health concerns you want to make me aware of?"

Nothing comes to mind, then I remember we're in a scene. This is not real life.

"I've been spending a lot of time in a dusty old house with a strange man," I tell him in my sweetest, most concerned voice. "It's been causing some terrible sensations."

"What sort of sensations?"

"I'm embarrassed to say, Doctor. I know I have a sickness. Please don't make me confess."

He hums, tapping his fingers against the clipboard. "We should probably make sure all this dust hasn't affected your lung capacity."

Mason fetches a stethoscope from the trolley, and listens intently while pressing it into the top of my breasts, over the soft fabric of my sweater.

"Take a deep breath for me."

There's no way he knows how to accurately take patient observations, and I'm unable to fight the urge to tell him what he's doing wrong.

"You're meant to hold it against my skin, I think."

Mason chuckles. "I'm aware, Miss. Do you think I'm a fake doctor or something?"

He reaches for something else, and the next thing I know, he's slicing through my top and tearing it open with his hands. He shoves it roughly to the sides and listens again.

I breathe deeply, certain the only thing he'll hear is my rampant heartbeat.

"Lungs sound clear."

Normally I wear sports bras for extra support, but the one I chose tonight is lacy and sexy, and pushes my breasts tight and high. Mason tugs the cups down over my nipples and gasps.

"No fucking way."

He stares down at me for a long time before picking up the dictaphone.

"Patient has pierced both nipples, and currently sports silver barbells." He clicks it off, lowers his voice, and hovers his fingers over them. "Can I? Please?"

"I might die if you don't."

"Put your arms above your head for me."

His touch is achingly tender at first. Rolling over one, then the other. I got them for me, and they feel amazing to play with, though the men I've been with before have shown little interest.

He slides the bars back and forth, the sensation sparking a new flood of heat between my legs.

"Those are so fucking hot."

He's never asked if I had any piercings. I wouldn't have lied if he did, but I'm pleased I could surprise him.

With his hands behind his back, he bends over and angles his head to lock eyes with me while he sticks out his tongue and circles it.

I watch him take it between his teeth and tug hard, sending a zip of pleasure shooting down my spine.

When I think he's about to move away, he spits on the other nipple, spreading it around with his gloved fingers. He examines me closely, pulling and pinching at my heavy, aching tits. I've tried to have nipple orgasms before, unsuccessfully. Maybe I just needed the help of a hot fake doctor.

Mason loses himself in playing with them, nipping me, sucking so hard I see stars. All I can do is lie there and take it, gripping the top of the bed until he tears himself away with a pained groan.

I watch him adjust the front of his trousers, fix his tie, and return to his observations. He clears his throat and stands tall.

"It's possible the patient's sickness is infectious. She appears to have the ability to possess those around her with her deviance. Future practitioners should be extra careful when examining her."

I press my lips together, giddy at knowing I'm having this effect on him, and I'm not even doing anything.

"Let's get your legs into position, and we can get started."

We haven't even started? What the fuck is he going to do to me now?

He leaves my chest exposed, and I fight the urge to cover myself up.

Mason steps between my legs and helps me lift my ankles onto the stirrups, securing them with a wide, buckled restraints. They're not tight, but I'm well and truly stuck. He then brings out a little rolling stool and positions it at the foot of the bed. Shame heats my skin knowing his face is level with my pussy.

"Ah, we might have a small issue with access here," he says to himself, rifling through the implements on the trolley. "Hold still, miss. This won't take a second. I just need to..."

He moves the lamp to one side, directing my gaze to where he slides surgical scissors between two gaps in my fishnets and neatly snips at the side of my panties. He repeats it on the other side and tilts his head.

"I need to make a few more incisions here," he says, dragging the sharp tip of the scissors down the seam between my legs. He cuts slowly, severing one section at a time, and I feel the gap pinging wider apart with each snip.

Even half in shadow, his face is the picture of professionalism. "We can reimburse you for these if you complete the paperwork at reception."

He swaps the scissors for something else and slips them beneath the lace that's already damp and sticking to me. Cold metal grazes against my hot flesh, and I yelp. The leg restraints rattle, and he glances at them with a perverse satisfaction.

"Lift your hips a little, please."

It's tricky at this angle, but I manage, and he yanks hard, pulling my underwear out through the slit he cut open. He lifts them up to his face, examines them, and drops them onto the tray before returning to his dictaphone, and his assessment of me.

"Pubic hair has been removed. Skin is soft and smooth."

I drove to the city to get a wax a few days ago, not wanting anyone local to know about the choices I make for my body. Not that I care about that when Mason is inspecting the most sensitive parts of me.

"Patient's cunt is swollen and soaking wet."

My hands cover my face. How is this so hot when it's so fucking mortifying?

"Clear signs of arousal." He presses one gloved finger to my entrance, scooping up the pool of liquid that's gathered there. "Fluid is sticky and sweet."

Oh my God, did he just taste me?

He continues his stroking, sweeping through my folds, up one side and down the other, never coming anywhere close to where I need him.

I shift to rest on my forearms, desperate to see more. With the dictaphone in one hand, he leans closer, watching how my body reacts to his torment.

"Clit is sensitive and throbbing." He taps it a few times, and when I whine, he has the audacity to laugh, and I think I might cry.

Fuck, I hate this, but I love it more.

"Cunt is clenching."

He keeps taunting me. Wiping my stickiness up and down. Pinching the sensitive skin at the tops of my thighs. Squeezing my labia. Pushing the flat of his palm against my aching hole.

"Patient appears desperate to be touched."

Desperate doesn't scratch the surface. My hips buck, hungry for his cock, his fingers, his tongue, literally anything as long as I have something inside me as soon as possible. I feel like all my wishes have been granted when he slips the tip of his pinky inside me.

"The ache she previously described can be witnessed when she clamps around the introduction of a probe, in this case a finger."

It's not enough, but I bear down on it anyway. He tuts at me, pulling it out and dragging it lower.

"Asshole is..." He moans, tapping it gently, circling, pushing against it. The pressure is incredible. "Pretty as fuck."

Even with my legs in the restraints, I twist and squirm, dying for more.

"Please," I beg, my eyes squeezing closed.

I don't know how much more of this I can take. My thighs are already shaking, but Mason pulls back, peels his gloves off and drops them onto the tray.

He unbuckles my ankles, then pulls the lamp back to illuminate my entire body. I catch the briefest glimpse of his face before he leaves the room without a word.

A howl of agony, a noise I've never made in my life, roars out of me.

It can't be over.

My breath hitches when I look down at the mess he's made of me, my nipples shiny and wet, my clothes torn, my pussy exposed and visibly aroused.

What the fucking fuck?

Only when I try to sit up do I notice a small cream envelope, tucked into the waistband of my skirt.

I rip it open, blinking to read the note on the back of his map.

Congratulations, Miss Laing. You're ready for The Round Table.

24

Jenna

Walking through Mason's house with no underwear on and my clothes ripped open feels obscene. I searched the trolley to see if he'd left something for me to wear, but I can only assume this is part of his plan. He wants me like this.

Dishevelled, distressed, and disoriented.

I'm in less of a hurry to find my second location, unsteady on my feet as I ramble the halls. Briefly, I wonder how much trouble I'd be in if I snuck off somewhere to give myself the orgasm Doctor Miller failed to deliver.

He grilled me at length about orgasm denial, and I agreed to everything, but now I'm so fucking horny I'm eyeing up the phallic bannister posts when I'm supposed to be heading upstairs.

I keep my head down as I climb, keen to avoid the judgement of the ancestors who stare down at me from portraits on the wall.

When I find the correct room, I rest my forehead against the door and try to control my breathing. Music leaks out from underneath it, a low, droning chant. It's the same music they play in the Ritual room downstairs.

My shoulders tighten. I wipe my clammy palms on my skirt, and try to pull the remains of my top back around me.

For me, the Ritual was the scariest part of the haunt. Tall figures in dark cloaks stood shoulder-to-shoulder in a long line. Watching. Waiting to strike. It was clear we were supposed to attempt to make it through the room without drawing their attention.

When Mum tried to rush it, one stepped in front of her and caged her in against a wall. She screamed her head off, and it's a miracle she didn't punch whoever was hiding underneath those robes.

One would be frightening enough, but being left alone with a whole row of them was worse. Beneath their hoods, they wore silver masks with cold black eyes. With the misted floor and hypnotic music, I forgot they were actors in costumes, and all I knew was I was petrified of being caught.

So I played their game and took it slow, but my bravado was entirely false. When I squared up to them, it was impossible to look away, and I felt drawn into a staring contest I'd never win. Anticipation clawed at my throat, and the longer we stood there in silence, the tighter it felt. When one finally lunged for me, I was no better than Mum, and I ran out screaming, too.

Mason knows that room scared me, but he also knows I love to be scared. Do I really want to know what's waiting for me on the other side of this door?

I know I don't want to leave, so there's no other option but to open it.

My heart leaps into my throat when I peek through the gap. The room is bathed in a red haze, and as I suspected, they're all here. Steeling myself, I step inside, and close the door behind me.

They stand in a circle, masks hidden by their huge hoods. Their cloaks pool around their feet, and they sway in time with the music. It's theatrics, but it works.

My body sways too, the frequency pulling at my cells and taking over my senses. It reminds me of the Gregorian chant audios I sometimes meditate to, and the way they make my brain feel smooth and my muscles soft.

"Welcome to the Round Table, Jenna." A chorus of voices, thin and ghoulish, drifts from somewhere far above us. "Step into our circle. Your fate awaits you."

I move without thinking, making my body as small as possible, as I slip between two figures.

In the middle of their circle is an enormous table, the top carved with dark lines and symbols, stars and constellations, an all-seeing eye. My palms skim over the surface, and I climb onto the table, my body moving as if driven by some other force.

I roll onto my back, and the figures appear to loom over me, their masks giving nothing away. The chanting soothes me, and my nerves evaporate as my body sinks into the wood.

I don't care about the state of my clothes or my body anymore. I'm here for them, an important part of their ritual. I know it, but then I remember I told Mason I didn't want an audience. I try to sit up, but two hands, sheathed in a black gloves, land on my shoulder and push me back down.

He stands by my head, his hands cupping my face.

"The spirits cannot be contained, but only two true hearts beat within these four walls," he says, his hands giving me a reassuring squeeze.

Mason.

Two hearts.

His and mine.

"Two souls, tethered by sin," he continues. "Tormented by desire. United in euphoria."

He steps back in line with the other figures, who I have to assume are a very convincing illusion.

Trust is important to Mason, he made that abundantly clear. I took him at his word, and he paid close attention to mine when I said I like the idea of being watched, but not the reality. What he's created here is better than anything I could have imagined, and once the panic subsides, the idea of all of these 'people' watching us has me writhing in anticipation.

I close my eyes and breathe deeply, waiting for the scene to unfold.

There's a clunking noise from somewhere beneath me, then the table begins to move, the top spinning slowly in an anti-clockwise direction.

My eyes fly open, and I twist my head from side to side, quickly losing track of Mason as the figures sway. The chanting gets louder.

Something, *someone*, grabs at my ankle, and I yelp as I spin out of reach. The table turns faster, and another hand reaches for my stomach, then my hair, then another, and another.

All these hands. Slow at first, then grabbing, pinching, pulling at my body. I'm moving too fast to make sense of it all.

Are there really only two hands?

They push my skirt up, squeeze my thighs, paw at my tits. It's the opposite of the doctor's slow torment. Frantic and overwhelming.

When they tear at my tights, I remember Mason asked for this. Fishnets are his thing, and I hope he loves what this looks like.

The music speeds up, and so does the table. My hands scrabble to grip the edge, hoping gravity will keep me here and not send me flying.

When I think I can't hold on any longer, the table jerks to a rough stop, and I scream in shock. A figure grips my ankles and drags me to the edge. My thighs are pushed wide, and I look up just in time to see him lift his mask and bury his face between them.

The hood of his cloak drapes over us both, and I can only feel the immediate relief of his tongue lapping at my hot, aching flesh.

The chanting gets louder, the frequency pulsing through my veins.

With greedy licks and hungry sucks, he growls against my core, and I feel the vibration of it ripple through me. I reach down to push his hood back, but he pins my wrists by my sides, his elbows keeping my legs spread wide.

He feasts like an animal with a fresh kill, his body gyrating as he gorges himself. I can't hear him over the music, but I can feel the hot, sticky mess he's making.

My back arches, and when my head rolls back, my gaze snags on one of the masked faces staring down at me. I look at them all, bucking my hips harder against Mason's mouth.

I know it's not real, but I don't care. I want them to see me, want them to witness him drink from my body, while they drink from my soul.

My pleasure chases the pace of the music, every muscle in my body shaking when his mouth clamps around my clit and he sucks hard. The sound of my orgasm drowns out the chanting, a guttural cry dragged from somewhere deep within.

A white-hot orb floats above me. Spectral. Pulsing. I throb with it, floating higher and higher, until Mason palms my cheek and guides my face towards his. I blink until he comes into focus, crouching by my side.

Did he just suck the fucking life out of me?

His forehead is damp with sweat, his mouth slick with me.

I roll closer, dying to kiss him, but he pulls his mask back down, and disappears from my line of sight.

Suddenly, the music stops, and all the cloaked figures slump to the floor, leaving me surrounded by nothing but piles of fabric.

Where did he go?

I crawl onto my hands and knees on the table and cry out for him. He can't leave me like this. It wasn't enough. It's never enough.

I need to be fucked like my life depends on it.

A bang makes me shriek, and the door I came in flies open, strobe lighting illuminating a brand new character. This one is in dark blue overalls and a hockey mask, and of course he has a bloody chainsaw in his hand.

How the fuck did he do that? And where is he getting all these fucking masks?

"Oh, Jenna," he cackles loudly. "Time to get up, darling. It's my turn to play."

He sounds deranged, even more so when he pulls on a cord that brings the chainsaw screaming to life. It's far too realistic to be a prop.

I scramble off the table, fighting the trembling in my legs as I stumble into the next room. I have no idea where I'm supposed to be going, but one of the staff doors is open in the corner, and it's my only chance to escape the man running towards me.

25

Mason

There's none of the grandeur of the house in these long corridors with their bare wooden floors. They're musty and dark until the strobe lights I set up with an auto-sensor start flashing again.

The chainsaw screeches and roars, but it's just a sound box attached to a rusty old one I found in an outbuilding. Jenna's brain might know she's not in any real danger, but her nervous system doesn't. It's shot to hell after coming on my face, and we're just getting started.

She tries every door she passes, but she doesn't know I've only left the one at the end unlocked. It leads to a staircase that will take her down two storeys, deep into the belly of the house, and the scene I'm most looking forward to. Or maybe it's the one after that.

Who am I kidding? I've been looking forward to all of them far more than she'll ever know.

I finally understand the meaning of a blood-curdling scream when the lights flash and she realises I'm right behind her. Her fear triggers mine, and I turn the chainsaw off, calling after her as her feet pound against the floorboards.

"Safeword, Jenna?"

"Green, motherfucker," she yells back at me, her middle finger held up over her shoulder.

Those two words have my basest primal instincts kicking up again. I want to chase her and tackle her to the ground and fuck her until I need to replace the floorboards.

God, I'm so fucking into this woman.

She nearly falls on her ass when the final door flies open. Scrambling to recover, she races down the stairs, and I hang back, knowing she'll need a second to get used to her surroundings. The bottom floor is underground, with wide corridors and arched rooms on both sides. They're old wine and beer cellars, cold stores for meats and fresh food from the days before refrigerators existed.

Untouched for years, they're mostly full of junk and creepy as fuck. The perfect setting for my damsel in distress. Jenna plays her role to perfection, and I can't wait to see how she handles it.

I stop the chainsaw noises, make my footsteps sound heavy on the stairs, then jump out at the bottom with the chainsaw high above my head.

"BOO!"

My voice booms against the old ceiling. Jenna screams again, and I stalk towards her in the strobing light. I'm in no hurry. My pretty prey is trapped, and she knows it.

She whimpers and slides down the wall, cowering in the corner.

Using the remote I have hidden in my pocket, I turn off the lights, plunging us into darkness. I focus in on her shaky, heavy breathing, and force mine to stay quiet. The sound is so fucking hot.

Fear thrives in the dark, and the air is thick with it. It's making me rock fucking hard. I don't want anything to be predictable, so I stand perfectly still, letting the tension build as she waits for my next move.

"Fuck you, Mason," she spits out eventually. It's so unexpected it makes me laugh.

"In a good way?"

"The best," she pants, and I hear her swallow hard. "What do you want from me?"

I want everything, forever, but I don't think that's what she's asking.

From another pocket, I fish out a miniature flashlight and shine it underneath my chin the way kids do when they tell ghost stories.

"You know the rules, Jenna. You can run, but you can't hide." I cackle loudly, loving how much fun it is to play these amped-up characters with unhinged voices.

She shields her eyes when I turn it on her and use the beam to scan slowly down her body. Flushed cheeks, heaving tits, shredded tights.

After cutting them open and ripping them with my hands, they're barely hanging on, but that's exactly what I wanted. I nudge her knee with my boot, and she spreads her legs wide. Her skirt rides up enough to reveal more of her, glistening wet.

Shining lights up her skirt is fast becoming my new kink. I wonder if there's a name for it.

"Would you look at that? What a filthy fucking mess you are."

Jenna slips one hand between her legs, moaning at the contact. My moans follow when she slips two inside herself and drags them out slowly. I love how much she's getting off on this, and I'm dying to see her make herself come, but it's not in the plan for this scene.

"Hey," I yell, stamping my foot so loudly it echoes along the corridor. She squeaks and snaps her knees shut. "You don't get to touch what's mine. Get up, slut."

26

Jenna

Anyone who's watched a horror movie knows you should never try to escape the killer by running upstairs, but I suspect you shouldn't let a masked man wielding a chainsaw chase you into the cellars of an abandoned old mansion, either.

Yet here I am, and I love it.

Like every room in this fucking house, things lurk in the shadows, dusty bottles and wooden barrels that seem to go on forever. In the middle of the room is a chair, almost throne-like, positioned underneath a single flickering bulb.

If Mason keeps this place, I swear the electrics are the first thing he needs to fix.

With his hockey mask still on, he nods for me to sit. I'm just getting comfortable when a crack of thunder and a flash of lightning has me leaping to my feet.

Mason pushes me back down, and the room fills with the sound of a heavy rainstorm. I wonder how he's doing all of this, but he's a master of props and special effects. This was never going to be a normal hookup. The thought makes me laugh so loudly it echoes off the old stone walls. Literally, *nothing* about this is normal.

"Been waiting a long time for someone like you to visit the house." He drags a finger down my cheek. "Someone to play games with."

"What kind of games?" I ask nervously.

My back sinks into the old velvet as he towers over me. It doesn't really matter what they are, I definitely want to play. He tosses something in my lap, and my eyes widen when I pick it up. A burlap sack.

"Put that on."

His harsh tone makes me fumble with the drawstring, but finally it's open and I pull it over my head. The material is rough against my cheeks, but it's breathable, and I can just make out the shape of him through the loose weave. Light flickers behind him, bringing his shadow in and out of focus as he moves around in silence.

He disappears behind the chair, and my head jerks when he lifts one of my wrists. The pad of his thumb strokes the thin skin there, a moment of tender reassurance, before he presses it down on the armrest. My other arm copies without thinking, fingers gripping around the curved ends.

The unmistakable sound of tape being pulled from a roll has my core throbbing, though I'm not sure it ever stopped.

"Please don't hurt me," I beg, playing the innocent victim just for him. "If you let me go, I promise I'll never tell a soul. You can trust me. I'll be good."

"Yes, you will."

He pinches my nipples hard enough to make me curse. Through the rain noise in the background, I hear him make a gruff sound, and then my tits are in his big, warm hands, his thumbs rolling and tugging at my nipples.

I wish I could see. Watching him spit on them in his makeshift surgery was such a turn-on, and knowing he's watching my body react to his touch is making me hornier than ever.

"Fuckin' tease," he mutters, dropping my tits and smacking downwards more gently than I'd like.

He pulls away and grips my face through the burlap. I can feel him breathing from the other side of it. So close, but not close enough. He shoves my face to one side, but it's playful, and I love the feeling of being his to play with.

His touch is rougher than when he examined me in the surgery room, but I'm not complaining. I've always wanted to be with someone who's not afraid to manhandle me. I want to be pinned down and thrown around and squeezed until he leaves marks. I already can't wait to see what state I'll be in tomorrow.

Next, he straps my ankles to the legs of the chair, holding them spread apart. When he's finished with his preparations, I hear his footsteps walk away, then another loud crack of thunder.

"Silly little girl," he tuts. "Look what you've gotten yourself into. Gonna split you wide open down here, and no-one will ever know."

The next sound is his chainsaw, and with each flash of lightning, his silhouette comes closer and closer. I try to take deep breaths and remind myself it's not real, but when I feel a buzzing sensation right between my thighs, I scream louder than I have all night.

It only takes a second to understand it's a vibrator, and I'm not actually about to be dismembered, but Mason's chuckle is pure evil as I thrash in the chair.

He holds it lightly against my clit. It's not enough, but somehow also exactly right. With my knees strapped, I'm powerless to do anything but sit here and take it, and I come shockingly fast, moaning my way through it.

I expect him to pull away, but he ups the speed and keeps it right there.

Oh god no.

Mason's pleasure dom is here to play, and I understand now that everything up to this point was just a warmup. My hips buck, my pussy aches, and though I know I don't stand a chance against him, my body still tries to fight it.

He presses harder, and when a second orgasm barrels through me, his laugh filters through the sack.

"You bastard," I hiss from beneath it. "Please, no more. I can't."

"Then you know what to say."

Red.

I don't even want to think it. Unless I use my safeword, he won't stop, so I press my lips together to keep my mouth shut.

"What a good toy," he says, and I know he doesn't mean the wand.

There's barely a second to focus before I'm coming again. My head sags forward, shoulders rolling inward. When the wave stays at its crest, I twist my head and bury my face in my shoulder.

"You can scream all you want down here. Nobody will hear you."

He says it like a threat, but I know it's a promise.

Mason knows how much I've longed for this, a chance to come loudly and proudly without holding back. I want it so much, but I'm not giving him what he wants that easily.

My moans become whines, so he grabs a handful of my breast and sucks at my nipple while massaging the buzzing head up and down my throbbing sex. The rhythmic motion pulls me closer to the precipice.

"Come on, Jenna. You can do better than that. Scream for me. Let it all out, you needy fucking whore."

He bites into my breast, sucking hard as I hiss through my teeth. I should hate this, but at this moment, I am a whore.

His whore.

My body was made for nothing but pleasing him. It just so happens that pleasing him means I have to keep orgasming until I'm on the brink of death, apparently.

He turns off the wand, but my relief is short-lived when I hear him spit, then feel it, hot and slippery, dripping over my clit. He spreads it around slowly, pinching me between his fingers, rolling, flicking, pulling.

It's too much.

Unbearable.

Everything.

All he gets from me is a series of high-pitched squeals, so he switches tactics, rubbing my clit from side to side with short, fast strokes that have me coming all over again.

When I'm done, he spanks me right between the legs, and I almost howl, but manage to pull it back.

"Oh, you think you're so clever, don't you?"

He squirts something—lube, I assume, and lots of it—between my legs, and I shiver at the change in temperature while it dribbles all over me. Then he's gone, somewhere out of reach.

The rain sounds make it impossible to place him in the room, but soon I feel the cold sensation of something hard and curved being pushed inside me.

He slips it in and out, twisting and turning, pushing deeper each time. Whatever it is, it's big, and it feels phenomenal. Nobody has ever used toys on me before. I want to see myself through his eyes, stretched and soaking and helpless.

"You will scream for me," he says, stern and impatient.

The toy buzzes to life inside me. I groan loudly and try to push it out to be a little bratty, but he just tuts and fucks me harder.

Mason presses his cheek hard against mine. His ragged, hot breath is primal in my ear.

"Scream, you pathetic slut."

He bites into my exposed shoulder, and when he puts the wand back on my clit, I lose the fight.

I scream and come, and I come and scream. My release floods every part of me, the pressure still somehow building while unholy noises roar out of my chest. I scream until my voice cracks, and the only sounds left are my wracked sobs.

He pulls the sack off my head, cups my face and lifts it to look at him. His mask is gone, abandoned on the floor in a pool of liquid I think might have come from me.

"Are you crying?"

His eyes search mine for reassurance I'm in no state to give. I gulp down air, unable to speak as he tenderly wipes the tears and drool from my face with his hand.

"Why did you stop?"

"Because you're *crying*." He kisses my cheek, one hand cupping the back of my head gently. "Why didn't you use your safeword?"

Did I forget? Did I even want to? I don't think I was even close to saying it.

"It feels so good. Please, Mason?" I beg. "More."

I don't know if I can even handle more than what he's already given me, but I'm desperate to try. He grips my jaw, then angles my head to run his tongue from my chin to my temple.

"Fuck, your tears taste good," he moans. "You're so pretty when you cry, baby."

Such a strange compliment, but it melts every part of me.

Deep in a place where nobody would find us, he's cracked me open, torn me apart, hunted for the things I've always tried to hide.

Yes, I'm half-naked and exposed and vulnerable, but I'm not afraid or ashamed. These aren't tears of sadness or fear. They're the rich tears of life and freedom and mind-altering pleasure.

Mason called me baby, and that one word burrowed deeper, tearing down my walls to reach the part of me that craves softness and care. It makes me cry harder, but he knows it's a good thing.

Working quickly, he rips open the ties at my feet, and reaches behind me to pull me to the edge of the seat. He pushes my knees wider and caresses the spot where my hip meets the top of my thigh.

"I love this part of you."

My skin is thinner there, dappled with stretch-marks I've had since my teens. He kisses them all, then switches to make sure I'm just as cared for on the other side. Then, his hands grip my calves, urging my knees up.

"Hook your knees over your hands. Keep them nice and wide."

He flattens his tongue and presses it against my entrance, dragging it from side to side. Thank fuck he removed the sack so I can finally get a proper look. His eyes never leave mine, and I watch him eat me so slowly, it's torture. He uses his tongue the same way he kisses, unhurried, then ravenous.

My thigh muscles twitch from the pressure of keeping them up, but that only heightens my pleasure.

Mason curls his fingers up inside me, pushing against the tender spot that feels so damn good. My body spasms again, and I give in to it, my mind slipping under as he unleashes an orgasm so powerful I swear I black out.

I scream until he pulls his hand away, muffling me with his soaked fingers. My tongue wants more, and he feeds them into my mouth, watching me taste myself and whimper the only word I'm capable of forming.

Mason.

27

Mason

Even in her wrecked and overstimulated state, Jenna is radiant.

Shattered and spent, a drooling mess, and still the most beautiful creature I've ever seen.

Her clothes are shredded, her make-up is smudged, and her thighs are still shaking from fuck knows how many orgasms she's had at this point. I'll give her a thousand more if she'll let me.

Before she arrived, I stashed bottles of water in each of the rooms. I uncap one and tilt her head back so I can slowly pour it into her mouth. Her eyes stay on mine, but I watch her throat roll as she gulps the whole thing down, wondering how well she'll be able to take my dick when I finally let her touch me.

"Check in with me, Jenna. Red, yellow, or green?"

"Green," she sighs, and my cock throbs.

"That's my girl."

She takes slow, deep breaths, in through her nose, and out through her mouth. I'm proud of her for grounding herself, getting her nervous system under control so we can keep going.

These scenes are only fun if she's genuinely enjoying herself, and if she were truly freaking out, we'd have stopped a long time ago.

I stroke her damp hair away from her face, waiting for her signal that we're good to move on. She nuzzles against my palm and hums softly.

"Did I squirt?"

"You sure did."

Her lips roll inward. "I'm so sorry. I didn't know I could do that. It never worked on my own."

She has nothing to be sorry about. It gives me a twisted sense of pride knowing I did it first. I want to be the only person who ever makes her feel that way. Saying it out loud is too much. I'm very aware I could scare her off by telling her how fast my feelings are growing, but she smiles up at me, and I think she knows.

She shifts in the chair, sitting more upright even though her hands are still tied.

"Are you ever going to fuck me?"

"Soon," I tell her, pressing a kiss to her forehead. "We have one room left. You think your legs can carry you there on your own?"

"I'll try my best."

I don't doubt her for a second.

"Open your mouth."

She's so compliant now, wrung out and putty in my hands. I find the key for the next room in the chest pocket of my boilersuit, and tap it on her bottom lip.

"Bite down."

The sound of her teeth on metal gives me a sick thrill. She breathes through her nose while I rip open the ties at her wrists. Even once she's free, she stays still, because she's the perfect plaything, just as I knew she would be.

"You'll count to thirty, slowly. Only then can you take that out of your mouth. Do you understand me?"

Jenna nods, and I bolt for the stairs. There isn't much time to get to her final scene, but I leave the door open so she'll know where to go. There's no need to make this next part harder after what she's just been through.

Stripping out of my boilersuit, I stash it in an old basket so she won't trip over anything, then pull off the t-shirt that's soaked in sweat from chasing her. Fuck me, that was fun.

When I reach the room at the opposite end of the house, the clothes I left out for us are waiting by the door. I change quickly, checking my tie in the mottled old mirror, and smoothing my hair down. The outfit I've chosen for Jenna is so her, and I hope she likes it as much as I do.

Slipping between the double doors, I push them closed behind me and pause to take it all in.

The Miller family's very own chapel never fails to take my breath away. Truthfully, I've wanted to fuck in here from the moment I first stepped inside, long before I even laid eyes on Jenna Laing. Who wouldn't want to rattle some demons in a creepy old church? It's kinky, and taboo, and if my ancestors are watching, I'm truly sorry for what they're about to witness.

Wooden pews line either side of the aisle, leading to an altar I've covered in black roses and battery-operated candles. They're not as good as the real thing, obviously, but the Miller house has survived hundreds of years of wear and tear. I refuse to be the fuck-up who accidentally burns it down because I was too busy thinking about my dick.

I take my place at the head of the aisle, my finger on the phone in my pocket, poised to press play the moment she arrives. When I hear the telltale creak of old wood, the spooky version of *The Wedding March* strikes up. The doors open wide, and I swear my heart stops.

My gothic bride.

The gown I picked is long and low-cut, made of layers of sheer black fabric. In the candlelight, I can just make out her beautiful curves underneath. Her other clothes are gone, but the fishnets are still there. Well, what's left of them. I love it all. Her full hips, heavy breasts, those shiny piercings that are burned into the back of my eyeballs.

Jenna bursts out laughing, then walks slowly, her bouquet held low, and long veil covering her face. When she reaches the top of the aisle, and takes her place opposite me, I lift it carefully over the back of her head.

"Dearly beloved, we are gathered here today..." the recording of my best church minister voice begins. She glances around us to make sure we're definitely alone.

The recording mimics a traditional ceremony, though the words fade to nothing because she consumes my senses.

All I can see is her, all I can taste is her, and all I can hear is my heartbeat chanting her name as blood crashes through my veins.

When the recording asks us to make our vows in the repeat-after-me style, her eyes widen.

"Is this real?" she whispers.

I shake my head, but when she says the words, I almost wish they were. My vows feel genuine, promises I'd gladly keep until death do us part, and long after that.

The rest of the ceremony is a blur, but I hear the last line loud and clear. "You may now kiss the bride."

Drawing her into my arms, she throws hers around my neck, and I get back to doing my new favourite thing. Kissing Jenna Miller.

Sorry, Laing.

Our tongues swirl in a kiss so erotic we'd never be able to do it in front of witnesses. Her bouquet tumbles to the floor, hands clutching at my suit jacket while mine grab fistfuls of her ass and pull her closer.

I run them up and down her back, weave them into her hair and tug hard enough to make her gasp. Her eyes are so bright and full I can see my own staring straight back at me.

"What now?" she whispers.

"Now you kneel for your husband."

While I'm focused on a partner's pleasure, I'm not even remotely thinking about mine. Those needs don't matter, and I don't let them get in the way of meeting all of hers. Sometimes that means I'm hard for hours, sometimes I don't come at all.

Pushing through the discomfort takes me to a headspace that makes the eventual orgasm even better. I can wait a long time for my turn, but I might have been waiting for Jenna longer than I ever knew. My cock is desperate for her.

I need her.

Now.

Jenna drops to her knees, her back straight and hands folded in her lap.

My goddamn perfect obedient little wife.

"Take me out," I tell her. "Slowly."

She looks up at me, a flicker of darkness beneath her sweet smile, as she tugs my shirt loose and my zip down. Her fingers hook into my waistband, and she drags everything to my feet, her head jerking back when my cock springs free.

Watching her see it for the first time is a fucking rush, especially when she licks her lips and leans in, but then she catches herself. She sweeps her hair and her veil away from her shoulders and holds her hands behind her back. Then she looks up at me, opens her mouth, and pushes her tongue out as far as it will go.

Stepping closer, I give my length a hard squeeze, and rest it on the tip of her waiting tongue.

"Don't move. I need a second to make sure I never forget this view." She stays perfectly still, eyes locked with mine. "You're so beautiful, Jenna. My perfect wife. Perfect whore."

Her lids flutter at my praise, and I buck my hips just enough to slide in another inch.

"Perfect mouth. Perfect skin. Perfect cunt."

She moans from the back of her throat, and her own hips twitch. I love how hungry she is, even after everything I've put her through.

"I want every part of you. Not just tonight."

I stroke the back of her head, then slowly push it down. She wraps her lips around me and breathes through it. I keep going until I can feel her throat tightening around my tip.

When I release her, she gasps for air, sticking her tongue out and waiting for me to guide it back in.

My good fucking girl.

"You okay?"

"Please, more," she begs. "Use me."

I stuff the head into her cheek and rub it through the other side, wondering how I got so fucking lucky. She works her way down my length with an appetite I can't deny. I go faster this time, pushing in deep, watching my dick get wetter with every thrust.

Her hands come up to grip the back of my thighs, pulling me into her as she takes me all the way. She gags around it, and I let go of her head, but she stays down for as long as she can before releasing me with a wet pop.

"Harder."

I grip the sides of her head and hold her still, my hips pumping in and out as she kneels there and lets me fuck her face.

I'm about to come just from the obscene noises her throat makes while she chokes on me. The mess she makes is even filthier, spit running down her chin and dripping onto her heaving tits. She pinches her nipples through the wet material, tugging on her barbells. I love that she's as into this as I am, and I get lost in watching her touch herself.

"Again," she gargles, wrapping one hand around my shaft and guiding it back in.

Her other hand cups my balls, rolling them in her palm and tugging just enough to remind me that even though I'm the one towering over her, she's in charge here.

She's the one who owns my cock, and possibly my fucking soul.

Her knees spread wider, her hips grinding against nothing. I wish I could go back in time and bring a toy for her to sit down on while she sucks me off. If she thinks our time in the basement was overstimulating, wait until we work up to filling all her holes at once. So many plans. I knew one night would never satisfy all of my cravings.

She strokes harder, her mouth open and greedy. "Mason, please. I want your come all over me."

I want that too, but not yet.

"Not until I feel you come with me buried inside you. Get up."

She scrambles to her feet and I guide her to the altar, bend her over it, and kick her legs wide.

28

Jenna

I hurry to gather the skirts of my wedding dress, lifting them up over my hips and holding myself open for Mason.

Behind me, he rolls on a condom, and takes great delight in teasing me with the tip. It's not enough, I'm dying to feel him. I try to wiggle back onto it, but his hand splays across my lower spine, keeping me pinned.

"Please?" I whine. It's embarrassing how much I need this. "I've been so good."

"Yes, you have, sweet girl. So good. You deserve this, don't you?"

His softer tone is almost hypnotic. I nod and lay my palms flat, rest my cheek on them, and wait.

Mason strokes the bare patches of skin my torn tights have exposed with a mix of feather-light touches and deep scratches. He drums his fingers between the apex of my thighs, a little tickle of my clit, a chunk of my ass between his teeth.

My need has me on the verge of tears, but then I feel him, *all* of him. Deep and warm and altering my brain chemistry.

He holds me still with his big hands, and if I died right now, I'd die so fucking happy. Bent over an altar and full of cock.

As *if* he owns a church. I'm truly living my best creepy weirdo life.

Mason fucks me slowly at first, and I let myself melt beneath him, slipping into that submissive headspace where I only exist for him.

His fingertips dig into my ass cheeks, squeezing hard and spreading me open. I hear him spit, then feel it, hot and slippery on my tight hole. He smears it around with the pad of his thumb.

"One day this will be mine too."

"All yours," I cry out. "I need it."

Mason picks up his pace, and I lean up on my elbows and arch my back. The new angle is even better, and with every thrust, my tits drag against the rough stone, the friction shifting me higher.

I fuck him back, and he groans loudly, bending to bite down on the tender spot where my neck meets my shoulder. A fresh rush of heat floods through me. I want it to leave a permanent mark. Maybe that's what I should get tattooed.

"You're gonna ruin me, Jenna. Turn around and lie back." He sweeps some candles to the floor to make more space. "Put your feet up on the edge."

I plant them wide, and he rubs his head against my clit. It's enough to make me come again, and it surprises him just as much as it surprises me. He stuffs himself inside and fucks me while I writhe through it. I didn't know this much pleasure was possible. It's relentless and overwhelming and I never want it to end.

Mason slows right down, watching the spot where our bodies meet. The look on his face is wickedly devilish.

"I said I wanted to feel you come with me buried inside you," he tuts. "Now you'll have to do it again. Show me how you play with yourself."

He pushes all the way in, hands cupping my ankles to lift my legs high and wide.

"Go on, baby. You can give me one more."

The words sound even better coming from him than anyone I've ever pictured in my head.

I stay propped on one elbow, and reach my fingers up to his mouth. He wets them for me, then I slip them between my legs. It doesn't take long, I can't even tell where one orgasm ends and another begins at this point.

Though the thought of touching myself for an audience has always been a turn-on, I've never done this before. Turns out Mason is the only audience I ever want.

"Oh, fuck, that's hot," he moans. "Look at you twitching on it. You trying to milk every drop out of me, greedy girl?"

My eyes roll back.

Why the fuck did I say yes to condoms?

I want him to fill me with cum until it leaks out between us. Want him to push it back inside me. Want to feel it seeping out of me for the rest of the night. Want him to lap it up and dribble it into my mouth.

That thought tips me over the edge, then I'm shattering around him, squirming and shaking as he holds me wide and pushes as deep as he can go.

Only when I stop rubbing does he move again, fucking me with rough strokes, taking what he needs to get himself there.

Then he pulls out and lets my legs back down. He tugs the condom off, and shoves his cock through a hole in my tights. I watch him press his hand down on it, thrusting it between our skin.

Now he's the one who looks possessed, and I'm utterly captivated by his determined focus on using my body to get off.

His eyes bore into the spot where his pre-cum coats my skin, but they flick up to mine when he hits the point of no return. We moan together when his warm release floods over the top of my thigh, his shifting to a whimper when the pressure gets too sensitive.

I reach up and cup his face, angling it downward so we can watch it run down the sides of my leg, pooling in the pockets of what's left of my tights, before it drips onto the floor.

It's the filthiest thing I've ever seen. And I've seen a lot tonight.

With a swipe of his thumb, Mason gathers some up, then paints my lower lip. An offering, a baptism, a who-the-fuck-knows-what.

"Mine," he whispers, leaning in for a slow, deep kiss.

When we finally pull apart, I rest my head against his chest and listen to the sound of his heartbeat. He holds me close, and we stay like that for a while, not ready for the night to end.

"You know I've wanted to do that since the moment I first saw you in these fishnets," he sighs into my hair. "Thank you for wearing them for me. I'll buy you more pairs."

And I'll let him ruin them all.

29

JENNA

IN MASON'S BATHROOM, I perch on the edge of the tub, too stunned to speak while he rubs lotion into the spots where his restraints left marks on my wrists. He's already washed and dried me and woven my hair into a braid.

This isn't aftercare, it's the aftermath of something fundamentally life-changing.

He kneels to soothe my ankles next. I'm sure I'll find more marks and bruises in the coming days, but they'll be the best kind of souvenirs.

"Do I get a sticker now?" I ask, and he looks up at me.

"What do you mean?"

"I survived the Miller mansion, right?"

His frown softens into a smile, and he kisses my stomach. "If you want a sticker, I'll get you a sticker. Anything you want."

Mason stands and slips an oversized t-shirt over my head, gently guiding my arms through the sleeves, before leading me to his bed.

I hadn't expected to sleep over, but I have no idea where my clothes are, and I'm not sure I'd manage to walk home, anyway. Mason knows it, and holds me the way I help our less mobile residents move around Crowmorne Heights. Which is good because my knees could give out at any second.

His bedroom is still decorated like the rest of the house, but the bed and sheets are thankfully modern, and we sink into the mattress in a tangle of exhausted limbs.

My head finds a comfy spot on his chest, and he reaches behind my knee to hook it up over his leg. From somewhere in the distance, a clock chimes. He counts each one off with a kiss on my temple.

"Is it really five in the morning?"

"Guess we lost track of time down there in the cellars," he says. "Your sense of time can get a little warped when you're so deep in pleasure."

He's not wrong there. He could have told me I'd been there for a week and I'd have believed him.

"You were perfect, Jenna. You did so well." His praise is a balm of its own. "How are you feeling? Do you want to talk about any of it?"

I shift to look up at him, and he rubs my back in long, slow strokes.

"The chapel was a little intense. I thought you were tricking me into marriage for a second there."

"No tricks," he smiles. "Only treats. I've just always thought it would be hot to fuck in a church, and it felt like a better fit than a sacrificial virgin scene."

My eyes widen, and he taps me on the nose.

"Ohhh, you're into that."

Another statement that's not a question. He just gets me.

"Um, yeah, I think I am." I stifle a yawn against his chest. "And the round table? All of those figures. How did you pull it off?"

"Come on now," he teases. "Can't give away all my secrets, but I can tell you there was some very strong fishwire involved."

I stroke the cut on his cheek with my thumb because we can't stop touching each other. "Might not recognise you when this make-up finally comes off. I swear I'm going to wake up tomorrow and this will all have been a dream."

"Well, Halloween is over. No more haunting, no more demons, but this..." he slips his hand underneath my t-shirt and squeezes my hip. "This feels like it could be an all year round kind of thing. If that's something you'd be interested in?"

My body freezes. We never talked about what would happen afterwards, and now I'm wide awake. I roll away and sit up, criss-crossing my legs and holding his t-shirt down between them.

"I thought this was a one-night only deal."

Mason sits up to face me, mirroring my position. He scoots close, covering my knees with his hands, and I feel his thumbs stroke soft, calming circles.

"I love this house, and I want to do everything I can to stay here. And I don't know what the future holds, but while I'm figuring it out, I'd love to keep buying your morning coffee and walking you to work. Maybe play a goofy boyfriend character for a bit."

"Boyfriend character?" I laugh, then cover my mouth. This isn't funny, and I'm not laughing at him, this is all just so unexpected.

"Yeah... but for real, Jenna. Can I ask you out?"

Even in the dim light, I can tell he's blushing. I've seen so many sides of Mason tonight, but the shy, flustered version was the one I met that first night, and it's the one I like best.

"That's very formal, considering what you just did to me."

"If you say no, I'll lock the doors and put you back in the cellar."

I uncross my legs and drape one over his, then the other. "Oh, that sounds really healthy."

He helps me slide into his lap, and my legs wrap around his waist like they've always belonged there. He trails kisses up my cheek and whispers in my ear.

"Come on, you'd love to be my sex slave, and you know it."

God, I really would.

"Tell me what goofy boyfriend stuff involves?" I brush my face against his like a sleepy kitten.

"Holding hands." He weaves ours together and kisses my knuckles one by one. "Twirling your hair. Date nights."

"I like the sound of that."

"Do you like scary movies?" His Ghostface impression sends a shiver down my spine, in the best way. I have visions of him chasing me through this house, before remembering that's literally what he's just done.

A fucking chainsaw.

It was unhinged, and brilliant, and scary, and sexy, and I'll never get over it. He tugs on my braid and snaps me out of my stupor.

"Mhmm, I love them."

"Then I'll build you a cinema. There's bound to be a spare room around here somewhere." He presses his forehead against mine. "We can brush fingers when we reach for the popcorn at the same time. Make out in the back row. Miss every ending."

Oh, what a life that would be.

"You should add an outdoor cinema next year," I tell him, stifling a yawn. "On one of fields. Screen all the classics like an old-school drive-in theatre."

"That's genius." He yawns too, and mine comes back with full force. "What movies?"

"You could show *Scream* and have actors in Ghostface costumes jump out and bang on the windows. Or *28 Days Later* and have zombies walking around in between cars. I think people would love that even if I think they're—"

He finishes my sentence for me. "Predictable and boring."

Mason Miller never misses an opportunity to show me how much he cares. He's always watching and listening and remembering the little details. Boyfriend Mason? Yeah, I think I do want to spend more time with that guy.

I run my fingers through his hair and kiss him softly. "Nothing predictable or boring about you though, is there?"

He strokes up and down my back, and we bounce more ideas around; for the haunt, for the house, for us. Mason's words are like a lullaby, and in my exhausted state my body sways backwards. He catches me, pulling me deeper into his lap.

I feel him half-hard through his boxer briefs, so I tip my hips and the friction makes us both moan. His hands sneak up my sides until he's cupping my breasts and rolling my nipples again.

"I meant what I said earlier, Jenna. That thing about wanting all of you, it wasn't just for tonight."

"I meant what I said, too."

"When?" His mouth hovers over mine, and I whisper against it. "Every time I begged for more. It feels like we're just getting started."

30

Jenna

One Year Later

Halloween has always been my favourite night of the year, but I have a feeling this one will be even better than the last.

Mason has been incredibly cagey with me for weeks, ordering packages that he quickly hides away, locking doors, and forbidding me from entering certain parts of the house at all.

His mind is incredible, and I've had the pleasure of helping him plan this year's haunt. The public one, that is. Whatever he's planning for our private one, I know I'll enjoy the surprise.

For closing night, I've picked a long, black, lace gown, not too dissimilar to the one Mason dressed me in for our scene in the chapel last year. This one has more layers, so he won't be able to tell I'm wearing a fishnet body-stocking underneath.

He's destroyed more pairs of tights than I can count this year, so I wanted to wear something even more special for him, and this one covers everything from the neck down.

When it arrived, it came out of the packaging bunched up like a tiny ball of string. I nearly lost my mind during the forty-five minutes it took to pour myself into it, so I'll beg Mason to take photos before he tears it off me.

There is probably not a room in the house that we haven't been naked in at some point, but now we're in spooky season, we try to keep our sexual proclivities to the bedroom. We might be deviants, but we're professional ones.

Mason's hard work last year paid off. The *'Will You Survive The Miller Mansion?'* experience had rave reviews, and sold out every night. By the time he settled his outstanding property bills, there was enough left to cover a few months while he decided on the next move.

A television company offered a nice chunk of money to use the house as a film location, and that paid for more upgrades. In the summer, he ran a drive-in cinema on one of the fields, and some of his London friends moved in for a bit to run a theatre camp during the school holidays.

Nobody would have blamed Mason if he had sold it, but he has a bond with this house, and sees its potential not only as a home, but as a space for all sorts of activities that benefit the community. I might not have known him before he inherited, but it's clear to see he belongs in Crowmorne.

I officially moved in in July, though I'd been here most nights before then, anyway. Sleepovers at my house were far too risky. With the way he likes to make me scream, we'd probably have woken my parents, my brother, and all the residents next door.

By day, I still work at Crowmorne Heights, but at night, completely unfathomably, I am somehow the newest Lady Miller. Or at least I will be when Mason and I get married here next summer.

Ha! Bet nobody in town ever had that particular theory about the future of the house.

One long summer night we sat on the terrace sipping drinks and poring over paperwork, piecing together more of the family's history.

When we found records of the marriages that had taken place in the chapel, Mason got down on one knee and told me he wanted us to get married there too, and he didn't care if it felt too soon.

Ours will be the first wedding on site, but our five-year plan accounts for up to fifteen in the summer months. We'll restore the ballroom to its former glory, furnish bedrooms for guests, and update the library for cocktail hour. We'll host Christmas markets for local small businesses throughout December, and, of course, the famous Miller haunt will be the highlight of the year.

It's been wonderful to see the house come back to life these past few weeks, with cast and crew coming and going for rehearsals and set dressing.

This year's haunt has been extended across two floors, and I've had a blast helping to source props and decorations. One room is home to the Apothecary, where an intimidating character named Ralph tries to push his mysterious potions onto guests. His display cabinet is full of jars of fake body parts, and on a shelf behind the counter is my prized collection of animal skulls.

Finally, my childhood hobby paid off, though Mum was not-so-secretly pleased to have them out of her house.

When we opened three weeks ago, I was a little sad I wouldn't get to experience the scares myself, but I've spent most of those nights in the Tavern, watching terrified guests crash through the door, fearing for their lives.

I was never going to be an actor, but as a child I often imagined myself spending my days in this creepy old mansion at the top of the hill. And with Mason Miller by my side, I'm right at home.

Epilogue - Mason

Many years later

My wife is hiding, and I cannot find her anywhere. Our version of hide and seek started as a sex game, but it's still our preferred pastime. We've chased each other through the hallways and secret passages of the Miller house more times than I can count, but I'm losing my touch.

I stick my head through the back of a bookcase, but there's no sign of Jenna in the library.

She's not in the wine cellar, or the kitchen, or her favourite spot on the terrace watching the sun go down. I've drifted through countless bedrooms, but eventually I find her, holding court on the front steps.

My Lady Miller is enchanting in her long black gown, and still the most beautiful woman I've ever seen.

"I thought we were playing hide and seek, my love?"

"You know I always end up in the laundry closet," she laughs. "But your great-great-granddaughter is in there with her latest boyfriend."

I rest my arm around her shoulder. Though I know she can't feel it, we both see it, and that's enough.

"Can you blame them? I told you it was a perfect spot for fooling around."

"And you proved it many, many times. Wait... Was that enough greats?" She counts them off on her fingers. "I lose track."

With the revolving cast of characters living in the Miller mansion, I myself lost track long ago.

Jenna and I were blessed with three beautiful daughters during our time here, who loved this place as much as we did. As their families grew and blended, the house found a new purpose, and became a commune of sorts.

More families arrived, and we welcomed them all. They decorated and renovated, added more buildings, planted fruit trees and vegetables. They filled the house with laughter and music, and danced barefoot under the moonlight. They raised each other's children, and the mothers raised each other.

In our twilight years, Jenna and I shared the same fear. We never wanted to say goodbye, not to the house, or to each other. When we died just hours apart, we were surrounded by more love than most people would know in a lifetime.

Who knows which fate or force decided we'd get to remain here in the afterlife. Never even believed in ghosts until I found myself here, but I'm grateful every day. Nobody can see us, but they seem to feel our presence when we get close. The family are all used to it, but Jenna and I never get bored of frightening new visitors.

"What are you doing out here?" I ask.

She raises her arm slowly, one bony finger pointing at the teenagers trying to balance a ladder against one of the trees that line the driveway.

"Making sure they hang the crow decorations properly."

"You know you can't tell them if they're not."

Happily, my wife can still roll her eyes at me from the beyond. "This is my Christmas, I can't think about anything else. It makes me happy to see our traditions continue."

The famous Miller haunt has been through countless iterations over the years. Some bigger, some smaller, and for several decades it took place in a corn maze grown especially for the season. We haven't hosted one for a while, and I know Jenna has missed the panicked faces and terrified screams.

Most of the members of the Miller clan inherited her love of all things spooky and scary, but young Charley Miller takes after me. He's often in the library, poring through historical documents, piecing together his own version of our shared history.

When he found tickets and stickers I'd saved from the very first haunt, he pitched a one hundredth anniversary edition, and the whole family said yes. I've watched with pride as they've pulled it all together, but nobody has been more excited than Jenna.

After the sun goes down, the gates open once more. We take our positions at the top of the grand staircase and prepare to deliver on the Miller promise of an unforgettable night of adventures.

"Happy haunting," I whisper, even though nobody can hear us.

Jenna gives me a knowing smile, remembering a moment we shared in this exact spot a lifetime ago.

"You're the best thing that ever happened to me," she says. Her hand reaches out to rub my cheek, and this time I'm certain I feel her touch. "Happy haunting, my love."

Bonus Artwork

Mason and Jenna art by
@poshotta

Bonus Chapter

If you're not ready to leave the Miller Mansion, enjoy this free bonus chapter where Mason offers Jenna a choice.

Trick... or treat?

Download your copy at https://BookHip.com/GGGHTVA

Acknowledgements

This book would not exist were it not for my dear friends Emily and Ellie. In October 2024, I suggested we book tickets to a Halloween haunt *'just to feel something'* and they both said yes even though we are nowhere near as bold as Jenna Laing.

We shrieked and screamed our way through that house, clinging to each other and trying to hide in every room. Ellie and I ended up in a pile on the floor with two strangers at one point (their fault, not ours!) while Emily tried not to die from how embarrassing we are.

Over post-haunt burgers, we talked about the book I was writing at the time (hi *One More Gift* fans!) and they suggested a book set around a Halloween haunt. Most of the details we cooked up that night are still in the book. She's on a date. The date runs off. She's left injured. The haunt actor is HOT AS FUCK and invites her back for a private night of spooky fun.

Emily and Ellie, thank you for being the best cheerleaders from the first line to the last. Next haunt tickets are on me, and I'll even throw in a fake crow.

A lot of other people helped make this book happen, too. Thank you to my beta readers Jill, Rachel, Beth, Alex, Wallis, Nicola, Katie, Danielle, Georgia, Hannah, Ali, and Ellie.

Thank you to Brooke, Jill, and Ellie for the additional support that gets books like this into the world.

Thank you to Aida Linnea for the stunning cover. We sat on this for months, and I was so thrilled to see everyone else loves it just as much as we do. Follow her on Instagram at @algart_

Thank you to Ellie at Lovenotes PR for ARC support, and the entire ARC team for your encouragement, kind words, and for championing indie authors.

Thank you to Meg Jones for content design. Working with you made this release so fun, and I can't wait to cook up some more ideas with you in the future.

And to Alex, for everything, always.

About the Author

Holly June Smith is a writer and romance addict who is constantly falling in love with fictional heroes and dreaming up new ones.

Originally from the North East of Scotland, she now lives in Hertfordshire, England, with her partner, their two children, and a TBR that threatens to crush her in her sleep.

You can find her online @hollyjunesmith, join her Patreon, join the Holly June Smith Reader Group on Facebook, or sign up for her mailing list.

Content Warnings

Please note that this book contains the following:

- A 'haunted' house
- Fake blood
- Kink exploration
- Medical roleplay
- Cloaked figures
- Mask play
- A chainsaw
- Overstimulation
- Restraint and blindfolds
- Degradation and humiliation
- Derogatory names (whore, slut, bitch)
- Use of toys
- Light CNC

- A (fake-ish) church
- Mentions of bullying (historic), deceased parents (historic), dead animals and decomposition (historic), and experimentation with occult (historic).

Please take care of yourself if any of these are triggering for you.

Also by Holly June Smith

Snowbound Secrets

Can I Tell You Something? (Hannah & Cameron/Mac)

See You Next Winter (Ryan & Kayla)

Sunshine Book Club Series

The Best Book Boyfriend (Kara & Luke)

The Worst Guy Ever (Hattie & Rob)

The No Rules Roommate (Megan & Ollie)

Standalone Romances

Just a Little Crush (Bec & Rennie)

One More Gift (Saskia & Henry & Casper)

Scary In Love (Jenna & Mason)

Printed in Dunstable, United Kingdom

69198065R00099